Dear Justine and Fiona,

I hope you like my little story.

Love and peace,

Martin
xx
x

THE WITCHETTY MEN

Special thanks to Ally Lott for your love and support; to Aaron and Jessamine Lott for your belief and typing skills, and to Pauline Lake for encouragement and proofreading.

Dedicated to the memory of Audrey Lott.

CONTENTS

Prologue

They stood alone. Horse and rider at the top of the moon-soaked hill, silent silhouettes beneath the lonely, burning stars. Below them, in the valley, the village lay sprawled and asleep, marked only by street lamps which hung like fairy lights dotted along the main road.

Looking out to the fields of corn, the man shivered slightly, brushed by a sudden cold kiss on the summer air. The corn bobbed and waved in the light breeze which whispered through the valley. The man seemed satisfied, though his horse could feel tension in the reins, and it stamped and flared its nostrils, champing impatiently at the bit.

The man continued to view the valley, his head filled with visions and plans, power and wealth and satisfaction. But there was something else, and it troubled him. An indefinable feeling. A feeling somewhere between tragedy and mystery which lodged in the pit of his stomach where it burned and gathered fear.

He dismissed it brashly. It was as irrational as the objections to his plans. They would be silenced and swept aside, for here was another village to crush. He laughed, false and loud, daring the feeling of doom to manifest itself. The laughter carried far into the night, far into the fields of shadowed golden corn.

A twitch on the reins, and they were off, thudding back down the valley at a canter. As the ground levelled, the man attempted to pull the horse back, gently at first, but harder in irritation when there was no response. With head down, the horse raced to a gallop, hooves sparking against flints which were scooped and flung into the night. There was terror in both horse and rider now as the fields flashed by. Terror etched on the man's grim face as he gripped so tightly on the reins that his knuckles became white; terror in the wide eyes of the horse as it fled from the invisible demons of the dark who taunted and teased, intimidated and menaced.

The horse veered from the path and galloped across a fallow field, rippling the grass which glistened like pearls. The moon loomed straight ahead, throwing strange shadows from the trees at the edge of the field. The man's face became beaded with perspiration as he continued to struggle for control of the twitching reins. His ears thumped heavily with the sound of his heart and the thud of hooves slapping against turf.

"*Faster, faster,*" the night shouted. "*Faster, faster, onward, onward!*"

Relentless speed.

The man sobbed into the saddle as the fingers of the first branches raked his body, and he screamed when the horse pulled up, throwing him through the air like a broken doll. When he landed, he twitched slightly and screamed no more. The wind whispered something and chuckled. And in the middle of the nearest corn field there appeared a circle.

1

The First Circle

"Come!"

Chief Superintendent Carl Downey responded unenthusiastically to the knock at his office door. His attention did not waver from the copy of *Sporting Life* inside which his head was buried while he casually studied form in advance of placing a few bets on the afternoon racing.

Sergeant Laurence Bailey entered the office smartly, and waited attentively, a couple of paces in front of the desk of his superior. An aroma of fresh coffee and stale tobacco permeated the room. This was added to by the vapour which rose from a steaming mug held at a slight tilt in Carl Downey's left hand, and curls of cigarette smoke drifting from a carelessly stubbed butt which rested on a pile of other butts in an ash-tray badly in need of emptying.

"Well, what is it, Laurence?" Carl Downey had recognised his colleague's knock, polite but firm, and the manner of his entrance, one which exuded quiet confidence.

"Another accident, Carl," Laurence responded. "This time a chap from the outskirts of the village named Alex Storey. Thrown from his horse, by the look of things. His body was discovered earlier this morning by one of the local farmers. Stone cold; probably been there for five or six hours at least."

Chief Superintendent Downey straightened his copy of *Sporting Life* and placed it in a matters pending tray where it joined the previous day's issue.

"That's the second this week." He spoke matter-of-factly, removing his feet from the desk and reaching to light another *Benson & Hedges*. "Anything suspicious to report on this one?" he continued.

"Not so far, Carl. The body has been positively identified by Mrs. Storey and a statement taken from the farmer. Forensics have checked the path the horse took. Nothing else involved, no chase, but it was going flat out alright. Judging by the spacing and depth of the hoof marks, they estimate close to forty miles per hour. The cause of death is likely to be the usual consistent with a high-speed fall—fractured skull, internal haemorrhaging...that sort of thing."

"You'll keep me informed if anything develops?" Carl Downey began to reach for the telephone.

"Of course, Carl," Laurence replied. "There was just one thing that puzzled me, though it's probably nothing."

"Oh?"

"Storey's horse was in such a distressed state when we found it that it had to be destroyed. The vet reported that the poor animal was completely blind."

"Well, that might explain the accident. Who in their right mind would want to go crashing through the night on a blind horse?" The Chief Superintendent gave a half-laugh.

"*No-one* in their right mind," Laurence sighed in agreement. As he turned to leave the room, he caught a glimpse of the local *Gazette*.

"That's out early, isn't it, Carl?" he asked.

"Hot off the press," Carl smiled. "Well, it's big news in the village and they need to increase their circulation. This will probably make the national press."

"Sounds important. What is it?" Laurence picked up the *Gazette* and began to read.

"We've just had our first corn circle," Carl continued. "Apparently they are fairly widespread in the South during the summer months, but that is our first, and, according to local spiritualist Madeleine Johnson, it won't be our last."

2

The Chosen One

Emily swung on the large wooden gate, hugging the top beam and staring downwards in a dream at the heat-cracked earth. The gate juddered. When it reached its full extent, she kicked against the ground and swung out in an arc until the gate clicked securely against the post. She rested in the heat, taking in the panoramic view of fields full of crops and of sun-scorched pastures. Men toiled below, tiny figures amongst the bales of hay. A tractor chugged and circled an outer field before picking its way back towards the farm in a shower of dust.

Beyond the outer fields, Emily could make out signs of activity in the neighbouring farm. This activity focused on one field in particular, and she was sure it was the field of corn that had caused such speculation and rumour in the village.

At that moment, Ben came into sight, scampering up the hill towards her. For him to have appeared so suddenly meant he had taken one of several short-cuts they had discovered over the years. He greeted her with a grin.

"Hi, Em! You'll never guess where I've been."

She tried to appear uninterested.

"Well?" he continued, still smiling that silly smile that promised to let you in on the world's biggest secret if you played along.

"I don't know, Ben," Emily replied. "Give me a clue."

Ben detected a hint of interest in the voice of his younger sister. He knew at once that he had her attention, and bowed melodramatically, sweeping the ground with his outstretched arm.

"A place large and round, filled with people jostling amongst the all-knowing, all-seeing corn, a place of magic and mystery."

"You haven't!"

"A place from which the crowds have now dispersed."

"You have!" Emily's eyes widened and excitement captured her breath.

"Oh, yes, but I have," Ben continued theatrically, "and despite a parental ban on visiting the area, and now public restrictions imposed by our neighbouring farmer, the secret of the first corn circle has been revealed to me."

Emily dropped from the gate and pressed towards Ben.

"So what is the secret?" She could barely contain herself.

Ben dispensed with the drama.

"Actually, Em, it's a trampled mess. I'm not surprised Old Gilbert has introduced a curfew. I can't see what all the fuss is about, really."

"The people must all be leaving now." Emily shielded her eyes with her hands and peered through the heat at a procession of sight-seers, meandering back along the distant farm track towards the shimmering main road.

Ben turned to look at the curiosity seekers as they filed away.

"You can still have a look, Em," he said. "We can sneak out after dark. No-one would know."

"But what if we're caught?" Emily wrestled with the idea, unable to decide.

"Caught by whom?" Ben smiled again. "I doubt if Old Gilbert will be patrolling the field at night, and Mum and Dad are such heavy sleepers that they would never hear us. Come on, Em. We've done it before."

Emily sighed, recalling previous occasions when they had fled from the house in mid-summer madness to run and hide in the fields and the shadows. An hour or two of daring. Time stolen from sleep. The escape route was an easy one. An old tree twisted past both of their rooms and it was simple to descend. The only hazard was where it passed under the window of their parents' room.

They had been caught once. Well, almost. One winter, when the snow clogged the trees and lay thick in the fields, they had spent an hour or so tobogganing in the moonlight. Because the escape tree had been too slippery to negotiate, they had used the back door. Ben, who came in last after returning the sled to one of the barns, had been caught by their mother who had got up in the night for a drink. He had pretended to be sleepwalking, and their mother seemed to have let it pass, though Emily was unsure if she was really convinced by Ben's act.

Emily agreed, weighing curiosity against risk. Curiosity tipped the scales.

It was cooler inside the farmhouse. Always a haven from the sticky heat of high pressure which had pressed firmly over the valley for the past two weeks. It was especially cool in the kitchen with its original stone floor—a floor which felt like icy marble in winter, but which caressed the feet like a mountain's cool stream in the fire of summer.

They sat at the large oak table, eating quietly while the news was broadcast on a small, portable television which rested on top of the fridge. At the mention of the village, their father rose from the table and turned up the volume.

The news switched to a location report from the village which suggested a possible link between the recent accidents and the sudden appearance of the corn circle. They listened intently as an interview was conducted from within the circle.

"So, Miss Johnson, what you are suggesting is that this first circle could be part of a sequence and that more will follow?"

"That is correct," the woman replied calmly, "but the appearance of the circles is not what concerns me most. It is the other sequence they may represent."

"Does this tie in with the fatal accidents that have occurred here?" The interviewer asked.

"I'm afraid I think it does—"

"No, really, I must interrupt at this point. There is no evidence whatsoever to support Miss Johnson's wild ideas." The camera cut to a police officer, also standing within the circle.

"Chief Superintendent Carl Downey, I take it, then, that you dismiss the suggestion of something sinister manifesting itself in our apparently peaceful countryside?"

"Absolutely," Carl Downey replied. "There is no indication of foul play in either of the recent accidents. They appear to be just that: tragic accidents. And this so called corn circle could just be the work of anyone. Probably practical jokers."

"Miss Johnson?" The camera returned to the woman who smiled gently, accepting the invitation to respond.

"I hope the Chief Superintendent is right. But I fear not."

"We'll have to leave it there. Thank you for your time, Chief Superintendent, Miss Johnson."

The news continued from the studio. Their father picked at the food on his plate with a fork.

"Damned interfering—"

"That's enough of that language." Their mother interrupted.

"Well, what do you expect? All this fuss and nonsense. Why can't they leave the village alone?"

"It will probably blow over in a couple of days. These things are soon forgotten," she continued.

"You are still forbidden to go there. Is that understood?" Their father glared at them until they both nodded.

"Sure, Dad," said Ben. "We know."

*

Emily lay in bed, listening to the familiar routine of her mother and father flicking the light switches, turning off the television, and bolting the heavy back door before retiring also. When all was still and dark, she listened as the farmhouse settled—the mysterious creaks and other noises which were only audible in the sultry heat of the summer night. Ben had explained that these sounds were the wooden beams shrinking slightly as they cooled after the heat of the day, and the creak of the stairs was a delayed reaction to the weight of Ben and herself on the way to their rooms. Emily wasn't so sure. She checked her watch and waited for Ben to appear at the window.

At eleven o'clock, there was a light tap. Ben sat astride the branch, smiling at her in the moonlight. She lowered herself from the window and dropped behind him. They crept towards the trunk of the tree in silence, stopping once when they heard their father cough and splutter in his sleep. Then he began to snore, and they continued their descent, dropping from the tree to land like heavy birds on the lawn.

The moon was on the wane, but when it peeped between the clouds, they were able to move safely away from the farmhouse without using the torch which Ben had wedged between his belt and jeans.

At the gate, Ben halted, and Emily drew level.

"What's wrong?" she asked.

He looked across the track and then ahead, snapping on the torch and sweeping its beam in a searching arc.

"I'm not sure, Em," he shrugged. "I almost feel as though we're being watched, but from a distance." He continued to play the beam from side to side.

"Stop it, Ben," Emily protested. "You're just trying to scare me!"

"I wouldn't do that, Em. Not tonight." He clicked the torch into darkness and they continued by the light of the moon and their knowledge of the land. Twisting from the track, Ben cut around fields and through groups of trees until they reached the neighbouring farm.

"What if Old Gilbert is keeping watch?" Emily whispered.

"We'll see him before he sees us," Ben replied, as they crept to the edge of the field which contained the corn circle. Emily shivered.

"You can't be cold." Ben nudged her.

"No, somebody just walked over my grave. Which way is the circle?"

Ben began to move cautiously around the corn field. As he did, something clattered above their heads in the branches of an oak tree. A rush of air, the beating of wings, and an owl flapped into the night, its sudden flight snapping part of a branch which tapped its way between other branches before thudding to the ground.

It startled them, causing a combination of panic to both run and freeze from fear. But the silence that followed was reassuring, and Emily pressed ahead to draw level with Ben. They soon reached the trampled path which led to the corn circle. It widened as they went. Ben played the beam of the torch across the ground and against the wavering wall which rustled in the moist wind that breathed through the valley. The circle was perhaps ten feet in diameter. The corn was flattened in whirling patterns. Emily felt another chill as she stepped inside. Then a rush of air seemed to escape from the ground, billowing out her jacket and tousling her hair.

"Em!"

Ben was startled. He stepped towards the circle but was unable to enter. An invisible wall shuddered and threw him to the ground. In anger and fear, he charged and was deflected even further, and when he stood, the circle was bathed in an eerie light and Emily was staring straight at him. But her stare was the stare of a statue.

"Emily!" Ben shouted this time, but his protest was whipped into the circle and absorbed.

"Kata Kaya, Kata Kaya!" The words echoed as though racing through a canyon. In Emily's mind, a picture slowly formed. An eagle soared through clear sapphire sky. Circling and crying, "Kata Kaya, Kata Kaya!" Strong face, the blink of an eye. Effortless flight. Now she was the eagle. Rising to meet the warmth of the sun. Embracing life. Powerful, all-seeing, all-seeking. Down in a dive. The rush of air stealing past her face. So fast she gasped. "Oh! No—stop, stop." The ground raced up to meet her, hurtling closer and closer.

"No—you must stop. Kata Kaya, you must stop. Please! Before it's too late!" she pleaded.

At that moment, the circle was broken, and Emily's mind grew dark as she sank to the ground.

"She is the one. She is the chosen one!" a woman cried, bursting triumphantly through the corn.

Ben raced forward to protect his sister. There were more voices, and movement in the corn. Ben turned, as if trapped. A group of men and women joined the first woman who kneeled and pressed a hand to Emily's forehead.

"We have waited. We have waited a long time for you."

"Leave her alone!" Ben grabbed hold of the woman's arm, but it was as rigid as steel. She spoke a string of strange words. "She will be alright, Ben. Kata Kaya."

The woman stood and led the group from the circle. Without uttering another word, they vanished back along the path towards the edge of the field, quickly swallowed by darkness.

"Emily, Emily, what's wrong?" Ben shook her slightly and she stirred. Her eyelids flickered, and she sighed as though in a deep sleep.

3

A Ring of Stones

The man stood at the centre of the ring of stones. He waited patiently, for the time had come. He could sense it in the pre-dawn air, and he could live and breathe the expectation. It was tangible enough almost to grasp. His tribe sat around the huge pillars of stone and they gasped when the first glimmer of fire appeared at the bottom of the sky. Today, the fire would be large and fierce. In the gentle dawn glow, the man appeared satisfied, and he looked about as the first wisps of vapour rose from the fields. He dropped his spear and raised his head to the heavens, marvelling at the softening sky which quickly cancelled the tiny ice-fires, erasing the night-time pictures for another cycle.

The tribe gasped again when the first light rising from the fire struck the tallest pillar, where it was refracted and distributed amongst the other stones. A dancing, dazzling beam, captured from the fire. An aura surrounded the whole circle like a gold and white halo. The tribe began to chant their praise to the fire god. Low and respectful, lest they should anger him. The man, however, remained silent, throwing back the hair from his forehead to reveal a head-band which contained a crystal at its centre. And when he judged the time to be true, he stepped into the beam. It hit the crystal and he was bathed in the colours of the spectrum. The beam entered and left the crystal, and now he closed his eyes and waited for the pictures. Yes—here they were! He laughed at the sight of another tribe dancing and waving their spears. These strangers were different in colour to his people and some wore bones on the outside of their bodies. This puzzled him and he longed to look closer. So real were the pictures that he reached out to touch, but he interrupted the beam and the image flickered.

The next picture puzzled him even further. A landscape of burning orange and green. Trees which he did not recognise, and ground that appeared to be burned by the fire god to an extent that he had never witnessed before. At first, he was startled by the strange animals. Like huge rabbits, they made him gasp in amazement. But after a while he became amused by their antics. Then one twitched, keeled over, and he could see a spear protruding from its furry belly. More spears rained on the huge rabbits, and then the dark hunters stepped forward, appearing from nowhere; so clever was their disguise. Now he understood and he nodded. These black hunters were men of the soil, and of the trees and bushes, and they had killed only what was sufficient for their needs, for the other large rabbits were spared.

The scene changed. Dark at first. The blackness slid slowly away to reveal a girl-child. The man was intrigued. Was this a child of the stars? She was dressed strangely in skins he could not identify, although the landscape was somehow familiar and he recognised the golden ears of corn. But why had the girl trampled the crops? He spat in disgust at her careless waste. If she was a god, she was not a good one. Now she was sending him strange visions.

A huge silver bird with wings that did not beat. And it was noisy, causing him to clasp his hands over his ears. The silver bird was taking her to a strange land. It had to be the edge of the world, for he could see the land burned by the sun god being soothed by so much water that he wondered how it could all fit in. Beneath the silver bird, the water was bruised by strange craft which headed towards the burned land. A tall pillar rose from the edge, and he marvelled at its uniformity. It was as high as the hills and perfectly formed. He wondered how many men it had taken to cut it out and roll it into position.

The girl-child reappeared. This time, she was lying on the ground, surrounded by a tribe dressed in strange skins. What could it all mean? Had the girl-child been sent by the gods to challenge him? What had he done to anger them? He looked closely at her face. Such perfect features. She was indeed a child of the stars. Unmarked. Both fragile and strong. Not stained either by fire or rain. And he would not forget her. He ripped the head-band away and strode from the circle. Angry with himself. Angry with the gods. And the fire continued to rise just like any other day.

4

A Broken Circle

"Heavens, I came as quickly as I could. How is she?" Ben was startled at the voice of a woman who entered the circle from the trodden path. Without waiting for a reply, she knelt at Emily's side.

"Mmm...obviously her first time. Ah, well—this should do the trick." She produced a small phial and waved it under Emily's nose. A sweet aroma, like summer flowers, filled the air. Emily stirred and opened her eyes, staring straight at the stars. Then she blinked and sat up.

"Ben? Who are you?" She turned to the woman.

"I'm Madeleine. Madeleine Johnson—"

"You're the woman on the news!" Ben interrupted.

"Very good, Ben," Madeleine replied. She offered Emily a hand and helped her to her feet.

"Now, how do you feel?"

"Strange," Emily managed a puzzled response. "I had the strangest dream."

"Hush." Madeleine placed a finger to Emily's lips. "Now's not the time. You must rest. We may talk tomorrow."

"Who were the others?" Ben asked.

"What others?" Madeleine turned to face him.

"There were people here just before you arrived. They entered the circle. I tried to stop them but something threw me back."

"I see," Madeleine sighed. "Then the circle was broken. No wonder you had such a bad time, Emily."

"They were led by an old woman," Ben continued. "She knelt over Emily and muttered some strange words..."

"What did she say, Ben? Do you remember?" Madeleine almost pleaded.

"Something about a cat and a car, I think." He shook his head.

"Kata Kaya! Just like my dream!" Emily exclaimed. "The man, the eagle..."

Madeleine became serious. "Then I was too late. I came as quickly as I could but I was too late."

"What do you mean?"

"A claim has been made, Emily. A link forged. You must return home. Go now; I have work to do." Madeleine's voice was kind and yet commanding.

"Call for me tomorrow," she added as they turned to leave the circle. "Fifteen Leed Street, eleven o'clock sharp."

When Ben and Emily had reached the edge of the field, Madeleine began to pace the circle. Every so often, she paused to utter words and to sprinkle the scent of summer flowers. Gradually, her pace quickened and the chant intensified. In the stillness of midnight's blue-black secrecy, she came to rest in the centre of the circle. With arms raised, she began to breathe deeply, concentrating on everything and nothing.

"Kata Kaya, break this link. Sever this circle from the sequence. Be gone with the dawn! Be gone, I command you!"

Madeleine stepped back, breathless with exertion, and a low, mournful wind blew softly across the valley. She shivered, for it was both cold and warm. It seemed to tease her and laugh. And a voice whispered to her. A voice which troubled her so that she turned and left the circle. Back along the path she retreated.

And in an adjacent field, full of bobbing corn, there appeared another circle.

"Ben, did you feel something?" Emily shuddered and looked back towards the corn fields, but the moon had slipped between the clouds and midnight was black as sable.

"No. What's wrong, Em?" he asked her.

"I'm not sure. Something isn't right. I feel Madeleine is in danger, but I don't know why."

"Stop there! Hey, you—stop!" The voice startled them.

"It's Old Gilbert! Run!" Ben whispered urgently.

"Hold on, now! Where do you think you're going?" he roared at them.

The first shot came as a warning. Twelve-bore lead shot scream- ing through the air far above their heads. They ran zig-zag, cutting a wild path over grass and between trees. The second shot whipped from Old Gilbert's gun and smacked into the ground immediately behind them. Then they were on home territory. Above the roar of her breathing and heartbeat, Emily heard the click of fresh cart- ridges being loaded. But they were safe now, diving for the cover of a corn field on their father's land. A few metres into the corn, they dropped to their knees and waited.

Within a minute, there came a clump, clump, and the scuffle of boots being dragged across parched land. Old Gilbert passed by, wheezing and muttering.

"Damned trespassers," they heard him complain. He paused, and for a moment, all was quiet. There came the tap and chink of metal upon flint as Old Gilbert lit his pipe. Then he turned and clumped away.

Only when the light haze of tobacco smoke had cleared did Ben move. The corn rustled as they brushed by and headed for home.

"That was close," Emily breathed.

"Yes, and he's probably woken the whole village," Ben com- plained. "I hope Mum and Dad are still asleep. But that's the least of our worries. We shouldn't have gone there tonight. Not after what happened, Em."

"I'm not sure that I know what really happened."

"It was scary, Em. When you were trapped in the circle, I couldn't reach you. You were there, but far away."

"I think that is how I felt." Emily frowned, remembering the strange vision. "I was the eyes of an eagle. I was an eagle. I was somewhere else, something else."

5

The Second Circle

The man scratched idly with the stick. He carved irritating patterns in the dust. Everything had troubled him since the appearance of the girl-child. He was still unsure what he had done to anger the fire god. And yet the harvest looked promising, for the fire had risen almost every day, and the rain god had blessed the land with his tears. The man vowed to make the corn offering worthy of such a harvest. Perhaps it would appease the god of cold and iron. The god who weakened the fire, and nipped their fingers and toes; the god who breathed icy wind, and turned the work of the rain god into icy white powder. And perhaps a sacrifice to keep the girl-child from troubling him. Maybe the gods would reach a compromise. He began to scratch the image of her face into the dust.

*

Emily awoke with a start. She could hear her father's voice in the hallway as he spoke on the telephone. It was too early for a business call, and she could hear his temper rise in what was quickly becoming a one-sided conversation.

"No, you can't just come up here. No, there isn't a body, just one of those circles. Well, if you do, you'll be trespassing."

He slammed the receiver into the cradle and rejoined their mother in the kitchen where the conversation became earnest but muffled.

Emily sat up. At the mention of the circle, she began to re-live the events of the previous night. They had been lucky to return undetected after Old Gilbert had alerted the whole village with his shotgun.

She dressed quickly, and tapped on Ben's door. He was already awake.

"I know, Em. I heard too. Let's find out what's going on," he said, as he joined her on the landing.

"Why are you two up so early?" their mother asked when they entered the kitchen.

"The telephone woke us, Mum," Ben explained. "What's all the fuss about?"

Their father glared at them. "Another circle. This time on *my* land!" he fumed. "How dare they?"

"Then that means—"

"That means what?" he retorted.

"Nothing, I just—"

"*Police have reported the discovery of another body in the village,*" the early morning news began on the radio, "*the third in ten days. There are no suspicious circumstances at the present time. There is, however, an unconfirmed report of the appearance of another corn circle. We will bring you right up-to-date at seven o'clock. On to today's weather...*"

There was a knock at the kitchen door.

"Yes?" their father snapped as he opened it.

"Chief Superintendent Carl Downey. My colleague, Sergeant Laurence Bailey," the man offered as an introduction. "May we..."

"I suppose so." Their father grudgingly stepped aside to allow the men to enter.

"What is it?" Their mother rose from the table.

"I'm afraid the body of Mr. Gilbert was discovered at first light this morning."

"Go to your rooms, please," their father ordered.

At the top of the stairs, they strained their ears to catch the fragments of hushed conversation.

"...no signs of a physical struggle, yet shots were heard and several cartridges found."

"We heard nothing unusual," they heard their mother say. "Poor Mr. Gilbert."

"It was probably a heart attack, but we're concerned, because he was obviously shooting at something."

"Probably trespassers snooping at his corn circle," their father said.

"His body was actually closer to the one on your land."

"So what are you suggesting, Chief Superintendent?" their mother asked.

"Nothing, ma'am. But if you *do* recall anything..."

"We'll let you know."

"What about your children? Did they hear the shots?"

"I can soon find out. Ben, Emily! Can you come downstairs, please?"

"Here we go, Em," Ben sighed.

"Well, what are we going to say?"

"Nothing. We heard nothing at all," Ben replied.

"But suppose poor Old Gilbert had a heart attack and died because of chasing us; I couldn't live with that on my conscience."

"We heard nothing, Em. Come on."

They shuffled nervously into the kitchen.

"The Chief Superintendent and the Sergeant would like to talk to you," said their father.

Emily listened guiltily while the officers broke the news of Old Gilbert's death.

"No, I'm sorry," said Ben. "I must have slept right through."

"Me too." Emily gulped.

"Well, thank you for your time. Sorry to have troubled you at such an early hour, sir."

When the door had clicked behind them, Carl Downey lit a cigarette.

"Let's get the report from forensic as soon as possible."

Sergeant Bailey raised his eyebrows. "The gun?"

Carl Downey nodded. "I've never seen metal so twisted. Melted as though it were plastic."

*

In the desert dust of Dreamtime, the slender figures danced around the crackling fire. The old man with a grizzly beard played his long pipe. Music from the wood. Music from the heart of the Earth, and around him the rhythm of life. The beating of stretched skins.

As the figures danced to fever pitch in the urgent wail and climax of sound and rhythm, one man daubed the rock. Since finding the head-band, the visions had come to him more frequently. At first, he had tried to shut them out, but now they seemed as natural as the day. So he painted what he saw. A face. The face of a girl. She was like the others he had seen. Strange and colourless. He laughed as he surveyed his work. Surely without colour meant without substance. She would be the consistency of water, slipping and trickling through his fingers. Then he looked at the silver bird, and below it to the shape on the water where trees without branches rose to the sky. He stopped laughing, and removed the head-band. The music and dancing stopped abruptly and faded with his smile.

6

The Sequence

"Which number was it again, Ben?" Emily asked as they turned the corner into Leed Street.

"Fifteen," he replied. "...eleven, thirteen—here we are."

They stood facing an ivy-covered cottage with a thatched roof, surrounded by a sweet-smelling garden. A fragrance of jasmine and lavender hung in the air, which was dotted with fluttering butter-flies and lazy, droning bees, busy amongst the flowers. Emily un-fastened the gate, and they approached the front door. The knocker was a miniature gargoyle, tarnished black by time, and above it, a small stained-glass window depicted a girl in medieval dress stand-ing in an orchard. Beneath the picture, a wooden plaque bore the inscription, "BLESSED WILD APPLE GIRL".

Before Emily had raised the gargoyle, the door started to open, and Madeleine's smiling face greeted them.

"Hello again, Ben. And how are you today, Emily? I'm so glad you could come." She stepped aside and invited them indoors.

"Good. This way, then." Madeleine led them through the hallway into a living room full of antique, Georgian-style furniture. The whitewashed walls were criss-crossed with dark oak beams, and decorated with brass charms and shiny horseshoes. On the mantel-piece, a row of joss-sticks smouldered, mingling with the atmo-sphere of aged wood and mystery. The neatly curtained bay window overlooked the spacious back garden. A freshly mowed lawn was bordered by flower beds, and the entire garden walled by a dark green privet hedge. At the centre there stood a statue of Cupid, poised with bow and arrow at the ready, and from his mouth, a fountain of water sparkled in the dizzy sunlight, collecting in a small, lily-covered pond beneath.

They sat together on a pink velvet couch, with Madeleine in the middle, where she poured tea from a steaming silver pot.

"Help yourselves to biscuits," she invited, as she handed them their tea in delicate china cups.

Ben began to relax, and sat back in the couch, but he was startled by a noise from above his head, and quickly jumped forward.

"*Cuckoo, cuckoo...*" the clock began, and Madeleine grinned at him.

"It won't bite, Ben. Here, sit down next to me." She patted the couch, and he smiled, and returned to his seat.

Emily wondered why they had been invited.

"I expect you are both wondering why I asked you to come," Madeleine began.

Emily looked astonished. Madeleine turned and gave her a knowing smile before continuing.

"I feared that time was against us. It always conspires. Last night confirmed my worst fear. I tried to prevent it. It normally works, but not now."

"What do you mean?" Emily asked.

"Mr. Gilbert. I'm afraid he was in the wrong place at the right time."

"Don't you mean the wrong time?" Ben interrupted.

"No, no, Ben. You see, the time is always right. He was in the wrong place. He really shouldn't have followed you. I summoned protection from the first circle. I didn't expect a second, but it is done, and I'm afraid there's no going back."

"I'm not sure I understand," said Emily.

"They are after something. Or someone. If the sequence is completed, they will return. And that could be disastrous." Madeleine lowered her voice as though afraid of being overheard.

"But who are they?" Ben implored her.

"The Witchetty Men. Keepers of early Earth, now returned to the stars. Their spirits here, laid to rest and dormant for so long, have been disturbed. Time's tunnel is beginning to twist."

"What about last night? What happened to me?" Emily asked.

"Only once in perhaps every thousand years are the conditions right, Emily. I think they have selected you as a channel. The corn circles form part of a sequence. They are like beacons which reach out to the stars, and when completed, the Witchetty Men may materialise."

"But why? Why would they come here?" Ben asked.

"They are being called by their kindred spirits," Madeleine continued. "The answer may lie in the deaths that have so far occurred. There must be a link. Of course, it would help if I could recognise the corn pattern, but it is too early, and I fear that when it does become clear, it will be too late."

"So the circles are the sequence," said Emily.

"Yes. According to what is written, the sequence is complete when a sign of the Zodiac appears. The circles will form a figure from the stars, but it could stretch over miles. There could be more already."

"Then the Witchetty Men could be here now. How would we know? What do they look like?" Ben began to panic.

"Slow down, slow down." Madeleine raised her hands. "They have not returned yet. It is said that no mortal may look at them and live. No mortal save for one: the girl-child, and even she may be in a time already gone, or in one yet to come. Who knows?"

Madeleine cleared the cups and left the room. From the corner of her eye, Emily detected movement.

"Something is out there, Ben!"

She scanned the garden, and as she did so, the privet hedge wavered.

"Calm down, Em. Don't be so jumpy," he said. But he shifted uneasily on the couch.

Madeleine returned. "Is something the matter?"

"Emily is imagining intruders in the garden."

"Then she is quite correct, Ben. Of that you can be sure. They have been keeping an eye on me for weeks now."

"Who are they, Madeleine?" Emily's eyes widened with fear.

"Members of the group who came to you in the circle last night. They may be after something, but I suspect they are just trying to scare me away. You see, they wish to harness the power of the Witchetty Men for their own use."

"But you're all alone here!" Emily was concerned.

"No, I'm not. I have Cupid. Watch!"

They looked into the garden, and as they did, the statue performed a slow pirouette and released an arrow which shot, like a bolt of lightning, into the hedge.

"Wow!" Ben exclaimed.

"What about the front of the house?" Emily asked.

"That's a different story. We'll worry about that some other time. Come now, it's time for you to leave." Madeleine led them to the front door.

"But what are we to do?" asked Ben.

"Be on guard," she cautioned, "and, Emily, if you are summoned to the circle, do not resist. I will try to be there also. In the meantime, be careful. You will know when to come again."

The door clicked shut, and they stood blinking in the sunshine.

"What do you make of all that, Ben?"

"I'm not sure, but there is something I'm keen to check out," he replied.

They paused at the gate and looked back at the house.

"And what's that?"

"The Witchetty Men," Ben continued. "I'm going to the library to carry out a little research."

The aroma of the garden was suddenly different, and Emily wrinkled her nose. It reminded her of something, but she couldn't be sure of what. Something sweet and menacing. And it was then that she noticed the gargoyle door knocker had vanished.

7

The Altar

The village was lazy in the heat. A pace of life that had never been quick was now at a slow-motion dawdle in the blistering early afternoon. The melting path moved slightly underfoot and a heat haze rippled above the black, sweating main road.

They stopped to buy drinks at the newsagent's. The stand outside displayed the headline of the Afternoon News: "LOCAL FARMER'S DEATH LINKED TO SECOND CORN CIRCLE".

Ben scanned the front page. There was a quote from Madeleine in which she mentioned publicly the Witchetty Men for the first time. Then, further down the page, there was another quote accompanied by a picture of a smiling woman.

"...the High Priestess claims further that the Witchetty Men are a friendly force, and have nothing whatsoever to do with the recent spate of accidents..."

"It's the other woman from the circle!" Ben exclaimed. "Look, Em!"

Emily peered at the photograph. "She looks familiar."

"But you were out cold."

"I'm sure I've seen her before, Ben." Emily's mind raced suddenly. The vision of the eagle once more. Poised to plummet towards Earth. A blur of wind and feathers.

"Em?" Ben jolted her. "What's wrong?"

Emily let her breath escape, relieved at the interruption.

"Nothing, I was just trying to place her face. I—"

"Will that be all?" the newsagent asked.

"Oh—just the two drinks, thank you." Emily replaced the newspaper.

The library appeared to be deserted, and an elderly bespectacled woman pointed them in the direction of the *Ancient History* section.

"Try looking under *Mythology* as well," she suggested.

Although it was a welcome relief from the heat, the old building smelt as musty as some of the old books which clogged the shelves. They drew a blank under *Ancient History* and turned instead to the *Mythology* section. Book after book failed to reveal any mention of the Witchetty Men, until, at last, Ben gave a loud whisper.

"Here it is!"

The book in question was a leather-bound, turn-of-the-century volume concerning Paganism. The pages were yellow and brittle.

"One hundred and twenty-five, one hundred and...thirty!" Ben almost wailed in disbelief. "Would you believe it? The section we want is missing!"

"There must be other books on the subject," Emily said.

"*There are no others*," a man's voice stated calmly.

Emily spun around. "Who are you?" she asked.

The man approached them slowly. He was middle-aged and neatly dressed.

A typical businessman, Emily thought.

"What do you want?" Ben faced him.

The man raised both his hands. "There is nothing to be afraid of," he assured them. "My name is Saunders. I represent the Director of a major construction company. My client is very keen to meet with you."

"Why should he want to meet us?" Emily was puzzled.

"Well, let us just say that there have been certain recent events which have caused him to be concerned. We think you might be able to help."

"You mean the corn circles and Witchetty Men, don't you?"

"That's right, Ben. Think it over and give me a call. I am sure we can arrive at a mutually agreeable arrangement." Saunders handed them both a business card.

"Think it over. But not for too long." He gave a quick nod, and left the library.

At the front desk, the woman whispered into the telephone. "... yes, Ursula. Yes, they are both here. No, he's just left; we are alone. Yes, I'm going to lock up now." She replaced the receiver and walked to the entrance. The old Yale lock clicked as metal scraped upon metal. Emily heard the sound.

"Ben, the old woman must be locking up," she whispered.

He was still staring at the man's business card. "How did he know my name, Em?"

"How should I know? How did he know where to find us? Come on, let's get out of here. This place is starting to give me the creeps."

The quiet and stillness of the library was interrupted only by the ticking of the grandfather clock—a monotone which punctuated the silence and made it almost deafening.

Ben rattled the door. Then he kicked it in annoyance.

"She's locked us in. I don't believe it. Surely she knew we were still here!"

Emily rang the bell at the unattended desk. The grandfather clock at the opposite end of the room chimed a reply.

"It's one o'clock. She must have gone to lunch."

"I'm not staying locked in here for another hour. Come on, Em. There must be another way out."

*

Chief Superintendent Carl Downey stared at the report from forensic. He turned the page, re-read the details, and stared again.

"Confidential, Carl?" Sergeant Bailey asked.

"Absolutely, Laurence. I want no details whatsoever released to the media. There has already been too much speculation for my liking. The pressure is on, Laurence. If we can't contain this, then it'll be over our heads. Don't get me wrong—I'll call for assistance if I need it. But I don't want it delivered unrequested. To put it unscientifically, the method used to melt Mr. Gilbert's shotgun was not of this earth. Twenty thousand degrees of heat achieved in a split second."

"And Mr. Gilbert?"

"Heart attack, Laurence. The old boy had had a dodgy ticker for years. He was also blind."

*

"This seems to be the only other door." Ben sniffed the air suspiciously before stepping into the passageway behind the front desk.

"Do you think we should?" Emily followed cautiously. "It's just like trespassing."

"We didn't ask to be locked in, Em," he replied. "We either find a way out or we sit around like bookworms for another hour or so until the library re-opens."

"Ben, isn't today Wednesday?"

"Yes. At least it was this morning."

"Then it's half day closing. The library is closed until tomorrow."

"That settles it. We have to find another exit." Ben strode the length of the corridor, spurred on by determined anger. The building had the same ancient, musty, and mysterious aroma even back here, away from the bookshelves. They arrived at a large oak-panelled door, which was secured by a black iron cross-bolt. Ben tugged at the dark metal rod, and it slid across with ease—iron on iron, echoing on wood. The door swung open outwardly.

"It looks like the only way is up." Emily looked at the stone steps which lay ahead, flanked by two stone pillars, which were grey and blotched by time.

"There's no light up there, Em." Ben faltered, forcing his eyes to adjust to the dusty gloom. "I'll go on ahead if you like. Wait here."

"No way, Ben. I'm not staying here on my own." Emily brushed past him and began to climb the stairs. Her feet slapped against the stone, finding contours which had been worn into the rock by centuries of use.

He followed her in a tight upward spiral, and when the light from the hallway had grown quite dim, the great oak door thudded into place. And when all was quiet, there came the sound of a key scratching in its lock, followed by footsteps.

"Whoever locked the door is on the inside!" Emily whispered urgently. "Come on!"

In the darkness, they held hands and continued to climb, fearful of the sound of following footsteps. Fearful even of the sound of their own anguished ascent.

It became suddenly lighter. A flickering light which cast weaving shadows on to the curving walls of stone. The steps widened and slowly opened to reveal a room which was lit by a circle of candles. The circle was two metres in diameter and contained thirteen equally spaced candles.

"I'm so glad you could come." The voice of a woman filled the room. There was a rustle of movement from the shadows, but no-one was visible.

"Please enter the circle, Emily." The command was both gentle and forceful, and Emily almost obeyed without thinking.

"Who are you? I can't see; you're hidden by shadows."

"But shadows are better than no shadows at all." The reply mocked and teased.

"Now you will enter the circle." The voice came from behind them. They turned defensively. It was the librarian, but she was dressed differently now. Cloaked and mysterious, just as the group of people in the corn circle had been. What was more disturbing, Ben thought, was the madness in her eyes. Fervent and extreme. The dangerous excitement of one possessed.

"Enter!" she hissed as she approached.

"Enter!" More voices echoed the command. Figures slipped from the shadows. It seemed they poured from the walls. Hooded figures shuffling and chanting, "Enter. Enter! Kata Kaya. Kata Kaya. Enter. Enter!" Their pace quickened as they circled the candles. A blur of silver and black. And Emily was drawn to the circle, ushered by the menacing woman from the library who swooped with her arms like an old, tired bird flapping through the musty air.

"Enter, enter! Kata Kaya. Kata Kaya!" Emily was inside the revolving madness, trapped by its urgency and fever. *"Faster, faster!"* The whole room was spinning. Sound and vision blurred as one. The image of the eagle. The voice of the eagle. She could feel its heartbeat and the tightness in its throat as it called. The swish of its wings as it trawled through the sky. "Kata Kaya!" Emily screamed the words as she sank to the floor of stone. Her cry dispersed the chant. The figures became still. They waited by the candles with heads bowed. And they hummed in a drone, like a choir of death.

The High Priestess entered the circle, flinging Ben to the floor so that he lay at Emily's side. The humming became louder. "Em!" he whispered. But she was far away, dancing across a summer sky. Then she began to hum.

At that moment, the altar became visible. Decked by candles. Stone on stone. The High Priestess spoke in an ancient tongue—words which Ben almost understood. Strangely familiar, but their meaning just beyond reach. Emily rose to her feet. She stepped slowly forwards, and lay on the raised slab next to the altar.

A figure approached and handed the High Priestess a crimson, velvet cushion. Now Ben understood, but it was too late. The strange words had left him mute. He was horrified at the sight of the long, cruel blade. Yet he could not pull away from the scene. He could not avoid the sacrifice. More strange words. A chanted response. Then the candles in the circle were put out. The altar seemed to sway. The dagger was swift and sharp. High and glittering, it sliced through the air.

*

The blood spurted on to the stone at first. Then it oozed and ran its course in a tiny crimson river along the edges of the slab. The man held the blade aloft, savouring the moment of the sacrifice, for this was sure to please the gods. Such a fine offering. And the time had surely been right. The vision had told him so. Some of the men in the tribe whimpered in fear, lest the gods be dissatisfied with the offering. The skies, however, remained calm. There was no spitting of fire or beating of angry sky-drums. All was well. The man nodded his head and the celebrations began. To start the feast, he scooped up the cup at the base of the altar, into which the blood had been collected, and drank it with relish. Gulping the warm liquid until it filled him with a new strength. He had not been troubled by the girl-child recently. Yes, all was well. He tore at the head-band and flung it carelessly into the air. He tossed it away as though he was disposing of bad dreams. It was with a light heart that he joined in the celebrations.

*

With a clatter, the object dropped on to the slab. The dagger sparked against stone. There was an uneasy silence. A smoky haze from the extinguished candles drifted across the altar.

"Can it be, Ursula?" The old librarian broke from the circle.

Ben shook his head, free from the spells of darkness. Emily also stirred and struggled to sit upright.

"It is!" The High Priestess was triumphant. "The vision is mine. At last I have the power!"

With arms raised, she turned to face the group of worshippers with a smile of victory. Then, with a surprising turn of speed, the librarian darted forward and snatched the head-band.

"No, Ursula!" she cried. "The vision is mine!" Her grey hands shook uncontrollably, but she managed to slip the head-band around her wrinkled forehead. "Yes, it is mine, and you cannot stop me now! Kata Kaya, come to me!"

35

Emily was fully conscious now and she swung her legs on to the hard floor.

"Get back!" the librarian screamed. "All of you!"

Emily halted in fright at the woman's reaction. The hooded group murmured and began to blend with the shadows.

"You fool!" the High Priestess sneered. "One as weak as you will not harness the power of the Witchetty Men!"

"It's coming to me. Yes, yes, I can see now." The woman's face appeared child-like as it was momentarily caught in the candle light which spread from the altar. She chuckled. "Yes, I can see. Thank you."

Then her expression changed. Her face became tortured with pain. "Oh! Oh!" she cried. "My eyes! Oh, my eyes!" She screamed and clutched her head, her fingers tugging at the head-band. "Ursula, take it off. Please!"

The High Priestess smiled mockingly and did not move. "You wanted the vision...well, now you have it," she hissed.

Now the woman was on her knees and facing the altar. She began to sob, then to writhe in agony. Convulsions wracked her frail body. "Help me! Somebody help me!"

Emily could bear the sight and sound of suffering no longer. She stepped forward and pulled the head-band away. It slid effortlessly into her hands where it felt hot and cold at the same time. Fire and ice together as one.

The High Priestess gasped and stepped backwards. "How could you...?"

The old woman began to crawl across the floor, still sobbing.

"Get up, you fool."

"But Ursula, I can't see...!"

The High Priestess was uninterested in the old woman's plight. She smiled. A smile as thin as water which ran quickly from her lips. "Emily, come now." She offered a hand. "Don't be afraid. It is our destiny. The chosen one *is* the girl-child." She edged forwards.

"Keep away from me!" Emily backed away.

"Just give me the head-band. I won't harm you, I promise." She began to chant strange words again.

This time Ben blocked his ears. "Don't listen to her, Em. She just tried to offer you as a sacrifice."

"Nonsense, Ben. You saw me. I was just bargaining for the vision. I wouldn't harm the girl-child. Now, Emily. Please give it to me. No...stop—don't do that. Don't put it on! You mustn't!" she shrieked.

Without knowing why, Emily slipped the head-band on to her forehead. It fitted perfectly. It felt as if it belonged. At that moment, the circle of candles re-ignited. The mustiness of the room was replaced by a sickly sweet odour, and the air began to move, to circulate.

"Ursula, are they coming?" the old woman gasped. "Tell me what is happening!"

But the High Priestess backed away into the shadows as the room swirled and began to roar. The candles flickered once more like tiny suns. They multiplied and shattered into specks of bright dust. Emily closed her eyes, but the room was still there. It was enormous. A vast swirling abyss of time and energy, racing closer, and then further. A myriad of stars. A rush of space. The hiss of twisting dimensions. The room raced and the stars blurred like drowning sapphires. Just as the rush of air seemed ready to engulf everything, the room burst into silence. The universe became calm, drifting gently on its dark velvet lake. Emily was gliding past the sun and past the planets. She recognised the one which lay ahead. Its dreamy swirl of white, blue, and green. It grew larger. Now it filled the whole room. It was the room. Through the damp clouds which soaked her, out into the blue below she fell. And the wind in her ears whispered, *Creation, creation, but we will be back.*

As a warning, the earth below erupted, spewing fire and smoke towards her. She could feel the heat—taste the acrid smoke which clogged her lungs. It was suddenly clear again. A vast ocean became land as she descended further. Mountains and trees raced by. "*Creation!*" whispered the wind. "*Treat us well or we will return.*"

The room soared to an enormous height, then plummeted. When all was still, Emily removed the head-band and blew out the candles. Smoke from the wicks drifted across the altar. The room was calm.

Ben rose slowly and shakily. "What was that?" he whispered.

"It was a warning. They were nearly here." Emily removed the head-band and stepped from the circle. "I think we should go to see Madeleine."

"But we've only just..."

"That was hours ago, Ben. A lot has happened. I'm not sure I..."

"Let's go, Em," he agreed, then added, "I wonder where everyone is."

As if in reply, they heard the sound of a key turning in its lock, followed by the clank of a heavy bolt.

"It's the door—come on!" Ben aimed for the stone steps. In feeling his way around the first curve of the wall, his fingers found a metal switch which immediately flooded the room with light.

"They've all gone!" Emily gasped. "But look what they've left behind." She pointed at twelve dark cloaks which were spread evenly across the floor.

They crept down the steps, pausing at the last bend. Ben leaned slowly forward. The great door was open. The way ahead was clear.

"It looks safe enough," he whispered, and they stepped into the passageway.

"It must have been that Ursula woman."

With an almighty crash, the door slammed shut. They spun around in terror, hearts thumping wildly. The bolt drew itself across, sliding forcefully into place. Without looking back, they fled towards the library.

At the front desk, they stopped. The library had been devastated. The whole room was a mass of books ripped from their shelves, and the splintered wood of what had once been shelves. Everywhere, the debris of torn literature was strewn around the sprawling room. The door at the front entrance had been ripped from its hinges, the frame buckled and useless.

"Come on," Ben urged.

They stepped around the mess and emerged into the street, blinking in the bright sunlight. "What do we do about..." Emily began, as the wail of a police car siren cut short her question.

"To Madeleine's." Ben broke into a run, and they sped from the shattered library, spurred on by the siren as it screamed its approach.

At the start of Leed Street, they paused to catch their breath, leaning into a wooden fence with hands on knees, gasping in the heat.

"Are you alright?" Ben breathed.

Emily nodded and began to walk. At number fifteen, she paused.

"Ben, something's wrong; this can't be Madeleine's house."

It was as if a dark veil had been drawn over the cottage. The rows of sweetly fragranced flowers had withered and died. The lawn was scorched and bald, and though the sun shone, Madeleine's house was cloaked in shadows. Emily stared at the open front door which swung idly, and it was then that she noticed the birds had stopped singing.

"What have they done? Where is she?" Emily marched angrily to the door.

"Careful, Em. You never know..."

"Ben," she cried, "look!"

The whole house had been ransacked and turned upside down.

"Madeleine! Madeleine, where are you?" Emily yelled.

They entered the living room. The furniture had been smashed and ripped. It was as though a whirlwind had forced its way inside.

39

"Even Cupid is broken. Look!" Ben pointed to the statue in the blackened back garden. The bow was snapped and the statue was at a crooked angle. The flowers here had also withered. Everything appeared to have had the life sucked from it, and while they watched, the sickly brown hedge began to smoulder. Seconds later, it burst into flames, creating a quickly spreading circle of fire. Fuelled by a sudden gust of wind, the whole garden roared and crackled, and ash and smoke billowed towards the house.

"It's a thatched roof; the whole house could burn!" Ben searched frantically for a telephone.

"Madeleine!" Emily called again.

"Let's get help, Em, before it's too late."

"But she might still be here!"

"They must have taken her. Come on!"

The roof was already beginning to smoulder as they stepped into the front garden. The first line of flames began to lick at the closely packed straw. Within seconds, the whole of the thatch was ablaze, and they were forced away from the searing heat.

"Well, I must say, you two have had quite a busy day." A heavy hand clamped down on both of their shoulders. "First the library, and now this."

8

Dreamtime

The man had walked into many sunsets to be at the edge of the world. He was still not sure exactly why he had come. The visions had continued to trouble him, yet their meaning was unclear. And the face of the girl on the rock had intrigued him. Her image had been sent—of that he was sure. He was convinced she had not come from inside his head.

From the cover of whispering trees, he looked out at the endless blue which stretched forever from the edge. The dust looked different to that which lay in the desert, and he marvelled at the white birds which hovered and then dived towards the moving, breathing water.

When he was satisfied that all was safe, the man emerged from the trees. He was short and brown, skin painted with the outline of bones. He was wise to the ways of the Earth, and he stood respectfully. And he waited.

The sun sank lower in the sky. He would not walk into the sunset on this day. As it bruised the sky and streaked the distant clouds, the pale ones came to him once more. So vivid this time that he could hear their strange cries. They were in craft which carved a path through the water, craft so unnaturally large, yet they provided support and prevented the pale ones from slipping beneath the waves.

The tribe without substance began to gather on the decks. They were dressed in different skins, a few wore brightly coloured clothes, but a majority wore skins the colour of mud, and they looked unclean. There was confusion in their eyes, and relief. Many appeared battle weary, but where was the conflict? He examined them more closely. Then he saw and nodded his head knowingly. The conflict was in their eyes. They were restless and unsure. But they numbered many.

Then one of them pointed straight ahead, straight at him, and their eyes seemed to meet. Just for a second, they were both aware of one another. It shook him cold. The eyes, the face—they were those of the girl he had painted on the rock. Now he understood. The pale people were coming to his land. The vision did not tell him when. Perhaps they were here already. The picture faded as the sun slipped over the edge of the day. He looked up at the pictures in the sky until the vastness made him feel giddy. Then he drove a spear deep into the heart of the dust. Let that be a warning to them. He thanked the head-band for its advice, then turned and vanished into the night. He had many sunrises to walk towards.

*

Harvey Stone watched the moving city from the luxury of his office penthouse. The city was grey even during the summer months, and it was greyer still when he had storm clouds in his eyes. People and traffic, all scurrying along with a pointless sense of purpose. They were trapped, going nowhere, and as their pace increased, so did their pointlessness. Harvey Stone sighed and returned to the reclining leather chair at his mahogany desk.

"I'm not the suspicious type, Saunders, but I can't take chances."

"Sir?"

"If this isn't a string of unfortunate...coincidences, then it is a deliberate attempt to block my moves. First Rogers, then Storey, and now Mr. Gilbert."

"The deal was nearly concluded, sir."

"I am well aware of that. However, the fact remains that it was not concluded. How are we progressing with Mrs. Gilbert?"

"It's a delicate time. She knew nothing of the proposals."

"Then lean on her, Saunders. Gently at first, but lean on her. We can't be delayed by a grieving widow."

"No, sir."

"Harvey Stone pointed to the Greenfields development model where houses, shops, schools and offices were neatly arranged on the village farmland.

"Phase One of the development will commence this year, Saunders. Do you understand me? This year, not next year."

"Yes, sir. Is there to be any further objection from the City Council?"

"No. A slightly modified proposal is being recommended at the next Planning and Development Committee. There are ways around the Green Belt issue."

"Modified, sir?"

"By money, Saunders. Company money. More to the point, my money. Now, how about these children from the other farm?"

"I have made contact with them, sir. I am confident they will co-operate."

"Good. And what of Councillor Jackson?"

"He is convinced the girl has some kind of ancient power. He was with the coven at the corn circle the other night."

"It's probably a load of old mumbo jumbo, but bring her to me anyway. I leave it to you to decide the method. Jackson is a meddling old fool, but he is useful. Keep him sweet, won't you? I need his vote at the Committee."

Saunders nodded. "Will that be all, sir?"

The telephone rang, and Harvey Stone snatched it from its cradle. "What is it, Molly? I said no calls."

He frowned. "Yes, yes, I see..." There followed a minute's one-sided conversation from the caller, before Harvey Stone concluded, "You will keep me informed. Personally. Thank you." He clicked the receiver into place and rubbed his chin thoughtfully.

"It seems we are up against the boys from the big league."

"Oh..."

"That was Head Office, Australia. A similar sequence of events has happened in Perth."

9

Orion, the Hunter

Bob Lewis swung the four-wheel drive Land Cruiser on to the dusty red road which cut through the wheat belt. In air-conditioned comfort, he surveyed the fields of golden fire which stretched for as far as the eye could see. The sky was completely cloudless, and the steady sun seemed to drip and pour its molten heat on to the land. Some ten kilometres down the track, he eased back on the accelerator, slowly bringing the vehicle to a halt. According to his calculations, the circle had been spotted by the surveyors at about this point. Then he saw it. A huge black dish in the wheat. A deep impression like a shadow pressing down. It had been spotted easily from the air and was just like the other two. Although several kilometres apart, they were idle dots on Bob Lewis' map of the wheat belt. Without really knowing why, he joined the dots together to form a triangle, and by each dot he wrote down the date of its reported sighting.

As he climbed from the Land Cruiser, the heat hit him like a furnace. A blanket of stifling air pressing and causing him to perspire immediately. How he longed for the relief of the afternoon sea breeze of Perth; for the refreshing Fremantle Doctor which swept in regularly from the sparkling Indian Ocean. There would be no such relief this far inland. He reached the edge of the circle after fifty metres. It appeared larger than the first two, and it had the same sickly-sweet aroma—only this time it was more overpowering. So strong, in fact, that it made him feel giddy. That and the combination of the heat. He stumbled towards the middle. The sun was directly overhead, and Bob Lewis began to fry underneath his hat. He estimated the diameter to be about twenty metres. It was as if a circular spacecraft had landed, settled into the wheat, and then taken off. He reached for his hip-flask, and tipped an ice-cold drink down his throat, wiping his mouth with the back of his hand. At that moment, he heard the whine of the Land Cruiser starter motor, followed by the sound of the engine firing into life.

"What the..." He could see the roof of the vehicle as it ploughed through the wheat towards him. It burst into the circle at full throttle and it was then that Bob Lewis' anger turned to panic, and he began to run. But his feet were heavy and slow inside the circle, and when he looked back over his shoulder at the advancing Land Cruiser, the last thing he saw before it flattened him was an empty cabin.

*

"And I suppose you really expect me to believe all this?" Sergeant Laurence Bailey sighed. "Well, I have to admit it's a good story, but you'll have to do better than that."

"But it is true, I swear it's true!" Emily insisted.

"It's no good, Em. He doesn't believe us," Ben said, before muttering under his breath, "and who could blame him?"

"Your father will be here at any minute. Shall we try again?"

Emily raised her eyebrows and sighed. "What about the librarian? Why haven't you found her? And Mr. Saunders—he knows we are innocent."

"The librarian is not at home. As for your Mr. Saunders, according to your story, he only witnessed the library when it was intact. Almost an hour before it was vandalised."

"The head-band, where is it?" Emily sprang from her chair.

"Steady on, young lady. Just stay where you are," Sergeant Bailey cautioned her.

"I'm sure I had it at Madeleine's."

"You must have left it there." Ben took Emily's hand and she sat down.

"I wonder where she can be."

"I hope for both your sakes that she wasn't in the house. Vandalism and arson are quite serious enough."

The telephone rang. "Yes, Miss Johnson. No, I'm relieved to hear that you are safe and sound. We've apprehended the culprits."

As the conversation continued, Sergeant Bailey's expression changed from one of relief to one of astonishment.

"But I saw it myself. I saw it happen. What do you mean, some sort of practical joke? Well, yes, I suppose so." He turned to Emily.

"She wants to speak to you."

Emily snatched the telephone. "Madeleine, I'm so glad you're alright."

"Listen, there's no time to explain. Sergeant Bailey will remember nothing of this as soon as you replace the receiver. I want you to come to me as soon as you can tomorrow."

"But the charges..."

"There can be no charges without evidence of a crime, Emily. Now you must leave." The line clicked and became a dialling tone.

Sergeant Bailey appeared confused. "Now, where were we...?"

There was a knock at the door.

"Come in!"

It was their father. "Now what's all this about, Sergeant? What have these two been up to?"

Their father stood in the doorway. His mouth framed a word, but no sound came. He stared at the Sergeant, who stared blankly at the figure standing in front of him. Both pairs of eyes glinted like sharpened steel. Then they softened like clouds. Their father blinked and shook his head.

"I'll let you know if I do, Sergeant."

Laurence Bailey awoke with a start. "If you do what, sir?"

"If I remember anything."

"Yes. Thank you, sir. Thank you for your time."

"Not at all." Their father turned and left the room without even acknowledging their presence.

"You'd better run along now."

"You mean we're free to go?" Emily asked.

Sergeant Bailey smiled. "Of course. There's no point staying indoors on a day like this."

"But what about the lib—" Ben began.

Emily nudged him. "Come on, Ben. The Sergeant said we could leave now."

As they closed the door, Laurence Bailey was suddenly troubled. He frowned and picked up the telephone. Then he sighed and hung up. Something wasn't quite right. "Just one of those days," he reassured himself, before returning to the pile of paperwork which covered his desk.

"Madeleine asked if we could call round for her tomorrow," said Emily.

"He didn't even notice us!" Ben wasn't listening. "It's as if..."

"Ben, she said the Sergeant would remember nothing."

"But the library. And what about Madeleine's house?"

"She said there can be no charges without evidence of a crime."

The High Street was deserted. The few shops the village contained were all closed. The library was closed. The library was intact.

In disbelief, Ben pressed his face against the glass. The debris had been cleared, the splintered shelves replaced, and the books neatly stacked.

"Is this what she means by no evidence, Em?"

Emily peered through the dusty window. All was as it had been. Even the twisted door in its buckled frame was repaired. And at the front of the desk sat the old woman. She rocked gently in her chair. Her lips moved but Emily could not hear her words. She stared towards Emily, but her eyes did not see.

Ben tapped on the glass. "Hey! Old woman!"

"Shh, Ben, leave her alone."

When they had gone, the old woman reached for the knife.

"It's coming to me. Yes, yes, I can see now." And when the grand-father clock had finished chiming the hour, the library was quiet again, except for the clock's gentle tick, and a slow trickle which dripped from the desk.

*

Emily was troubled in her sleep. The events of the past few days trawled across her mind, dragging dreams and reality from both the deep and shallow of her subconscious.

The eagle called once more, but this time his wings dripped with blood. The blood of an innocent blowing in the wind. She saw a spear flung by a lonely figure, deep into the sand of a distant shore; only to be kicked and snapped by an untidy crowd. There were people in boats. People laughing, people crying.

She saw fire and bellows. The clink of metal. The smell of war and destruction. Hope, futility. A map, a triangle. A closing sequence, stars bursting. Accelerating, slowing. There was a shape in the mist. It was sky through the clouds. The stars were trying to burn their cold fire through the high bank of cloud. One, two, three. A triangle. There were more stars but they were hidden.

Frustration turned into fright.

"Girl-child, oh, girl-child..." It was the High Priestess mocking her.

"Run now. Run until your heart bursts."

In her dream, she obeyed, chased by the creatures of the night. Hot pursuit, blind panic; she ran and screamed. A backwards glance caused her to trip. She fell into a deep chasm. A spiral of twisting stars. There was nothing to hold. The universe raced by.

Emily awoke with a bump. She checked her watch. It was 3 a.m. The house was still. The air was so warm and so heavy that the night felt like a tightly drawn net. She stood at her window from where the stars lay sprinkled in the sky like an ocean of diamonds. When she looked for more, the sky became even more enormous. A dizzy multitude of far-away suns blinked and shimmered.

Then Emily recognised the triangle of stars from her dream. There it was! They formed part of Orion, the Hunter. She closed her eyes in concentration. It was the same formation as the map. She was sure of it, and, without really knowing why, she clicked on her bedside lamp and made a sketch of the pattern.

Her sleep was again troubled. This time, Orion flexed his muscles and strode across the heavens. He was searching while she watched. He reached down from the sky. His agitated footsteps were thunder in the clouds. Emily was frightened. It seemed Orion knew she was watching. He looked at her and came closer. Now he was kneeling. His face pressed nearer, so near that she could almost reach out and touch...nothing. He roared and thundered away, stamping his great footprints over the sky so that the other stars shook and began to fall. Like fireballs melting from space, they rained on to the Earth. Orion bellowed his fury. But when he returned to his position, the bombardment ceased. All became calm once more. Then a star rolled from his belt and tipped from the sky. As it erupted in flames on the ground, Emily awoke. Sunlight streamed through her window, catching and holding the particles of dust which danced their strange, eternal dance around the room. She breathed a sigh of relief. Then Emily glanced at her sketch of the stars and she gasped, snatching the paper from her bedside table. It was impossible, yet it had to be. Her hands shook slightly as she gripped the sheet. She had drawn three stars.

Now there were four.

*

The man lay broken and bleeding in the sweet-smelling bracken. He licked at the blood which oozed from his swollen lips. They had come without warning. A tribe of invisible metal warriors astride great beasts. They could not be cut or slashed, and their long knives had been the glint of death for many of his people. Now the village lay smouldering. The small mud huts were flattened, the best of the women taken. But he had to be strong. And he had to find the headband. He was sure it would have warned him about the attack. He was sure it would have helped.

The sun warmed his blood-soaked back, but, when he stood, his broken skin cracked and bled again. Some men lay face-down in the mud. Some lay face-up, staring at the sun; staring at nothing. There was an uneasy calm. As he stumbled towards the Summoning Drum, he saw it in the grass. Trodden by the feet of the metal warriors' carriers, it was half-embedded in the soil. He dug feverishly with his fingers until the earth released its treasure. Then he placed it on his forehead and beat the drum. It was time for a new beginning. It was time for revenge.

10

The Museum

"But the whole house was burning!" Ben insisted. "How could...?"

"Regeneration," Madeleine said softly.

"And the library?"

"The same. More tea?"

She poured without waiting for a reply. "It's just as well that you left me the head-band."

"It was an accident. I must have dropped it," said Emily.

"An accident? No, I don't think so."

"Are you suggesting it rebuilt this house and half the library?"

"It is a great source of power, Ben. This is part of the Witchetty Men's power." She tapped the head-band lightly. "Unfortunately, it isn't the only one. Ursula and her misguided followers still have the power to harness the dreams and visions."

"How many head-bands are there?" Emily asked.

"It's difficult to say. They were used in ancient times. The Witchetty Men could communicate advice and warnings to the Old Leaders. They left Earth when they deemed mankind fit and capable of looking after the planet. At the time, all the dream-bands were supposedly collected. A few may have been left behind, but this one, according to what you have told me, was sent. It was summoned, demanded by Ursula in exchange for the girl-child's safekeeping."

"Then I really am?"

"There can be no doubt about it, Emily. You are a very special young lady. Look after your dreams. They will guide you."

"Last night, Madeleine, I dreamed of the sequence! It's Orion, I'm sure. He leaned out of the sky and it rained fire. I drew three of the stars and when I awoke there were four. Look!"

Madeleine unfolded the sheet of paper. Then she frowned. "There are only three, Emily."

As the sheet turned over, a shiny speck fell through the air and hit the carpet with a sizzle and a smoulder. Madeleine nodded. "That was the fourth star. It looks like part of Orion. There is no news of another circle yet, but if we can plot Orion on a map, we should be able to pinpoint the next circles. Of course, we don't know which star is next in the sequence."

"They have warned me, Madeleine. They are nearly here."

"Good heavens, they have been *nearly here* for years. This time, they are just...closer. There is a great deal of conflict. The Earth is uneasy. Too much has been destroyed. The ways of the Earth have been ignored. Then, as now."

"How can there still be conflict in the past?" Ben was curious.

Madeleine smiled. "Time is not for the consumer—it is for the consumed."

Ben shrugged. "I'm not sure I know what you mean."

"I don't know that I know, either. Come, I'd like you to meet an old friend of mine. He's the curator of the City Museum."

As they left the room, Cupid turned and fired an arrow. His aim was true, but the arrow passed through the target as if it had no substance. He reloaded the bow.

*

A 2CV was crouched in front of the house. They climbed in and were soon leaving the village. The car groaned as it leaned along the weaving country roads. Its noise startled the birds in the fields, and they took to the air, swept upwards like black, beating dust. The sun, which shone like a spell over the countryside, dimmed when they approached the grey outskirts of the city. They were soon clogged in the arteries of roads which led to its slow beating heart of cement and stone.

There were high-rise office blocks and shops, metal railings, and glass-walled buildings. Traffic rumbled, doors slammed, faceless people rushed by. Madeleine aimed for a precious parking space and they walked the short distance to the Museum. Ben wrinkled his nose at the smell of the city. Gone was the sweet fragrance of the countryside. Instead, the choking fumes of diesel and petrol engines, and the smell of fast food and cheap perfume.

The Museum was one of the city's oldest buildings. Previously, it had served as the Town Hall. Now the walls of its stone corridors were lined with drawings and paintings depicting the city at various stages through history. The Council chamber and Committee rooms contained displays and objects of local interest, dating back as far as the first evidence of settlement in the area.

"Why, Madeleine! How wonderful to see you!" The elderly curator greeted her. "And you've brought some young visitors." He smiled at them warmly.

He took Madeleine by the arm and the two engaged in a hushed conversation. After a few minutes, they returned.

Madeleine introduced them. "Was it like this, David?" She indicated towards the head-band which Emily held.

"Hmm...I'll need a closer look if you don't mind. Thank you."

He turned the head-band over in his hands. "It is of the same age and style, though not identical to the one which was stolen."

"Stolen!" Ben exclaimed, and his voice carried along the corridor.

"As I was telling Madeleine, the Museum held a piece such as this until the break-in last night. Whoever it was knew exactly what they were looking for. They took nothing but the head-band."

He turned to Emily. "And I understand that you are its special guardian."

"I think so."

He laughed. "Well, I'm sure you'll do a splendid job. Shall we?"

He invited them to follow and they were shown into one of the Committee rooms.

"This is the display from which our head-band was stolen."

The room contained a reconstruction of part of a mud hut village.

On the walls were hung an array of tools with descriptions for their use.

"As you can see from our time-chart, they were a quite primitive race until the period this reconstruction represents. It seems that the age of metal arrived quite dramatically. Then there was no holding them back. All the major discoveries occurred over a relatively small time scale. Fire, metal—even the wheel. Discoveries...or perhaps introductions." David stood by a large drum at the centre of the room.

"This is what was known as the *Summoning Drum*. It was used by the head of the village to summon his people."

To emphasize the point, he struck the stretched skin. The sound boomed around the room. The resonance vibrated through their bodies—the bass tremble locked around their hearts.

David struck the drum again, but the third beat was struck by a different hand. It belonged to a short, bedraggled man clad in bloody skins. His black eyes stared straight at them, and straight through them. He threw back his head and raised both arms in a gesture to the sky.

"Kata Kaya—eagle god—give me your vision. Seek out the men of metal!"

The room was alive. The walls, floor, and ceiling rippled like water and vanished. Now they were outside. They were in the mud hut village. There was a smell of smoke and earth, and something that was hard to define. Madeleine shuddered. It was the essence of war —the smell of death and destruction, of exertion and despair. At the next beat of the drum, there was movement. A group of men slowly assembled around their leader. They were weary and wounded from battle, yet their eyes also burned brightly. They waited uneasily for the man at the drum to speak.

"Look—he has the head-band!" Ben pointed.

"Shh—they'll hear us," Emily whispered, "won't they, Madeleine?"

"I'm not sure," she replied. "Let us watch quietly, just in case."

"From the flame will come a harder blade," the man spoke. "My warriors, you have proven your courage beyond doubt. Soon will be the time for revenge. From the stone and the flame will come this."

There was a gasp as the man snapped a sword from the air. But one man from the group spoke.

"How shall we know there will be more?"

"This is sent as proof of the method. A higher flame, a colder blade. Stronger and sharper to slice through their metal skins. Our answers are here. The only way is forward."

The man stopped speaking. He moved from the drum and stepped towards them.

"Don't move," Madeleine warned.

He stopped in front of Emily. He looked puzzled. It seemed he stared straight at her. Emily felt his presence, his breath, his confusion. He turned to face his men.

"She was here also!" he cried. "They have sent the girl-child to look over us. Be she good or evil, have your wits about you, my men!"

The man's words blended with the tone of the drum. The air sang like steel stretching. Then all was still, and it was David who stood at the drum. They were back in the Museum, but just for a moment, the aroma of the village lingered.

"Were we there, Madeleine?"

"I think they may have been here, David." She spoke quietly as if her energy had been drained suddenly.

"He called to the eagle god. Kata Kaya has been in my dreams." Emily moved towards the drum as she spoke.

"Kata Kaya was their most powerful god—their overall keeper. Provider of sight where they could not see," David explained. "The head of the eagle appears on almost all of their tools, and, without exception, on their weapons."

"Where did the sword come from?" Ben asked. "And what did he mean by *a higher flame, a colder blade?*"

"I think we may have just witnessed one of man's technological advances," said Madeleine.

"It could have been a reference to the smelting process. Greater heat to extract a different metal from the ore. In this case, perhaps a superior metal with which to produce a stronger blade."

"But he was helped, wasn't he?" said Ben.

David agreed. "And through Emily we have been privileged enough to see how man may have made one of his important advances."

Emily ran her fingers along the Summoning Drum. "He must have seen me, so I was there."

"You could have been then. He could have been now." Madeleine turned to David. "And now we have to take a look at Orion."

He nodded. "Their hunting god."

"Emily feels he may be the Witchetty Men's corn circle sequence."

"Orion would seem appropriate. But he could stretch for miles. Let's see, shall we?" David led the way to his office. From a bookcase, he removed an Atlas of the Universe and a local map which he spread on the desk.

"We'll mark the circles that have appeared locally."

"Here." Ben pointed. "And here. That's ours and Old Gilb..." He stopped at the mention of the dead farmer.

"Where is the third?" David asked quickly.

"Right up here," Madeleine replied. "It preceded these two."

"Now we'll take a look at Orion." He flicked through the Atlas. "Here he is."

"But there are so many stars," said Emily. "Surely there can't be a corn circle for each one."

"I doubt it, Emily. I think we should concentrate on the major stars which make our Hunter. There are seven, see? These four for his limbs, and the three in the middle which form his belt."

As David paused, Madeleine spoke his thoughts. "That's it!" she cried. "We have Orion's belt."

"But I drew a triangle," Emily protested.

"Yes—but this is a triangle. The belt isn't straight." Madeleine linked the sites of the corn circles.

"If we plot the remainder on the same scale, we have our sequence." David began to calculate.

"What happens if Orion doesn't appear to scale?" asked Ben.

"I would prefer not to think of that possibility," David replied. "Of course, there is another problem."

"Oh?" Madeleine's eyes locked with his as they pored over the map.

"He is crossed by the celestial equator."

"Meaning what, David? Don't talk in riddles."

"Meaning he is visible from everywhere on Earth. We may not be the only point of attack. Australia would be a prime candidate."

*

There was something about isolation which made the man feel even closer to the Earth. It was an indefinable feeling, yet he was at one with nature. Both master and servant, observer and participant. Like a lonely ship crossing an amber ocean, he retraced his steps from the edge of the world. Away from the tribe without substance. Their arrival was surely imminent and the prospect distressed him greatly. He doubted their intentions. If they had any respect, they would keep away.

That night, as he slept by the fire, his dream was so vivid that it made him cry out. He nearly rolled on to the glowing embers. Spirits were rising in their hundreds and thousands. Faces upward turned, blank faces with open mouths, skins of red and yellow, pale and dark, all floating away from the Earth. Behind them fell a trail of dust in great sweeping clouds. The dust of their dreams. As it drifted, the world appeared through the gaps. A scarred world; blackened and bruised. Twisted by heat. A curious aura pulsing around its dead crust. Then came laughter. Menacing laughter which stung his ears so that he covered them with his hands and rolled with pain.

The spirits rose towards a figure. It was a man clad in a tattered black cloak. In one hand he held a box, topped by a red, flashing button. He threw back his head and laughed.

"Holocaust!" When the figure in black extended a hand of invitation, the man cried out and awoke, shaking with fear.

Dawn somehow revealed more than a new day. Something had changed, but whether it was a change within the world or himself, the man could not be sure. He felt violated. The Earth had been betrayed, and he felt guilty. The man of the Holocaust was not of the same tribe as the ones without substance. Yet he had their same pale colour and eyes which did little to veil an untruthful tongue.

Before the sun became too strong, he arrived at the caves. He began to paint. It would take many days to draw what he had seen.

*

"This is probably the only reliable book on the subject." David removed a leather-bound, gold-embossed volume from the safe. "And it is one-of-a-kind," he added.

"It's hand-written!" Emily exclaimed. "It must have taken ages to write."

David nodded. "Probably the work of a lifetime."

"A book of centuries—condensed centuries." Madeleine marvelled at the attention to detail.

"More than a book, Madeleine. Much, much more."

"In what way?" Ben asked.

"Read the first line."

Ben cleared his throat. "In the beginning, the Witchetty Men created..."

"But that's Genesis," Emily interrupted.

"Of course. A Bible has to start at the beginning."

"Bible..." Ben struggled to accept the possibility.

"Religion, history, morals, guidance. Even the Ten Commandments. It's all here," David explained.

"Isn't it blasphemous to imply...?"

"There are many beliefs, Emily. Perhaps one god with many names," Madeleine suggested. "It helps to have an open mind."

David continued. "There are references to corn circles appearing at the time of significant historical events. Most, be they good or bad, are interpreted as either a blessing or damnation from the Witchetty Men. Here is a section regarding the future. The author must have had access to one of the head-bands. There are references to the Black Death, the Great Fire of London, Apollo 11, to name just a few. Oh...here we have the discovery of Australia. This one is odd—it's called Altricia. A man clad in black robes holds the box with the flashing button. Could be anything, I suppose. Volcanic eruptions, floods, the Great Wall of China, World War II."

"How old is the book?" Ben asked. "It looks quite new."

"Carbon dating was dismissed because it would destroy the sample to be analysed. The material is a mystery to me."

"Not of this earth?"

"Quite possibly, Madeleine. But to answer your question, Ben, I would guess it to be at least two thousand years old. Of course, it could be older. Much, much older. There is another fascinating section concerning the universe. Quite remarkable accuracy—well beyond the power of the naked eye—yet these star-charts, and the map of our Solar System, were compiled centuries before the invention of the telescope."

"The planets have different names."

"In this map, yes, Ben. Only Earth is the same," David agreed.

"And there are ten planets," Emily pointed out.

"Clavius," said David. "An orbit of four hundred and thirty-two days, placing it between Earth and Mars."

He flicked through the pages of the book, and, having found the relevant chapter, began to read aloud.

"*...and before the Day of Judgement, there appeared a series of circles to warn the people of Clavius. Yet they continued to mistreat that which they had come to cherish. When the sequence was complete, the Witchetty Men then returned to Clavius.*

"*'You are creating your own destruction. See how the people of your sister planet cherish the Earth. Return to the old ways. Bow down before us and be saved.'*

"*But the people of Clavius would not return to the old ways, nor would they bow down and be saved. In anger, they attacked the Witchetty Men, and in retaliation, Clavius was flung from orbit to wither and die in the icy exterior of the Universe.*

"*They were saddened at the loss of Clavius, and vowed to keep a closer watch over the Earth.*

"*'Let our spirits rest now, but let them make contact with us if they are disturbed. In the meantime, we will offer advice from afar. In one generation, a child of the stars we grant to further safeguard that which must be cherished. Kata Kaya. May the eye of the eagle—the flight of the eagle—be with her. Now our work is done.'*"

David closed the book slowly.

"Now we can all understand why the sequence must not be completed," said Madeleine. "We cannot run the risk of incurring their wrath. Ursula..." She bit her lip. "Damn her—she must have taken the Museum's vision-band."

"What will she do?" asked Emily.

"She will encourage their arrival. She means to harness their power. We have to be ready for the next circle."

"Can we stop it?"

"I don't know, David. But with Emily's help, we can try."

"You said there might be a link between the deaths."

"Yes, Ben—the spirits were only to make contact if they were dis-turbed," Madeleine replied.

"Then we should..." He turned to Emily.

"Yes."

"We should contact this Mr. Saunders." He took the business card from his pocket. "This could be our link." David read the card. "*Harvey Stone Construction Ltd.* What is he after, I wonder?"

"He wants us to help him," Emily replied. "He knows about the corn circles and the Witchetty Men."

"I think we should go. We'll see you soon, David. Thank you."

"Take care, Madeleine. All of you, take care."

11

Harvey Stone

"I'm afraid Mr. Stone is in a meeting at the moment," the Secretary apologised. "Did you have an appointment?"

"No, but he is anxious to see us," Madeleine replied.

"We're from the village," said Ben. "He wanted to talk to us about the Witchetty—"

"Shh, Ben!" Emily nudged him.

The Secretary removed a list from a file on her desk.

"Ah, yes. You must be Emily and Ben. And you are...?"

"Madeleine Johnson. I'm a friend of the family."

"Well, if you don't mind waiting, I'll get a message to Mr. Stone. I'm sure he won't keep you too long. Excuse me." She left the room.

There were two Perspex-covered models in the office which aroused Ben's curiosity immediately. Perfect miniature developments, just like towns appeared when viewed from an aircraft. The attention to detail was astonishing. Apart from the buildings, there were cars, trees, and even people.

The first development was called Island Village, Rottnest, Western Australia. But it was the second model which caused him to gasp in horror.

"What's wrong, Ben?"

"Madeleine, it's the village. Our village! Look—they want to build on all the farmland."

They gathered around the Greenfields Development model.

"Well, I must say our Mr. Stone means business."

At that moment, the Secretary returned. "Mr. Stone will see you now. This way, please." They were shown through a set of double doors, and into a much larger office.

"Miss Johnson, Emily, and Ben, sir."

The chair behind the desk swivelled so that the man faced them.

"I'm Harvey Stone," he greeted them. "I'm so glad you were able to come. Please take a seat."

"Mr. Stone. We have just been looking at the models of your proposed developments."

Harvey Stone smiled. "Awful, aren't they, Miss Johnson?"

"Well, yes."

"They are the proposals of one of our clients. We were simply acting as consultants. Our recommendation is that the proposals be withdrawn. On planning issues alone, they are completely unacceptable."

"Then you're not building on our farmland?" Ben asked.

"Not at all." Harvey Stone smiled. "The village is quite safe."

"Mr. Saunders said you were concerned about the Witchetty Men." Emily came straight to the point.

Harvey Stone retained his smile, though his eyes shifted uneasily. He clasped his hands together and leaned forward.

"The recent accidents involved people who worked for me. Now, they could either be tragic coincidences, or somebody could be threatening the Company for some reason."

"And you suspect the Witchetty Men, Mr. Stone."

"Miss Johnson, I have to keep an open mind. My responsibility is to the Company and its shareholders."

"And to the environment."

"I am a property developer. My schemes, be they large or small, are designed to complement their surroundings."

"How did you find out about the Witchetty Men, Mr. Stone?" Emily was curious.

"I am kept well informed on many issues. I have heard about your...shall we say, special gift?"

"And?"

"And if it is possible to find a peaceful solution..."

"If it is the Witchetty Men, we are not in a position to bargain with them," Madeleine snapped. "Someone is disturbing them, and, if it is you, then I suggest you revise your plans."

"There are no major plans locally, Miss Johnson."

"They don't have to be local. If I were in your position I would delay all development proposals."

"That would be impossible."

"They are coming, Mr. Stone," said Emily. "It could be you next."

"What about Mr. Gilbert?" Ben asked. "He didn't work for you."

"No—but he was part of the Greenfields Consortium."

"You mean he wanted to re-develop the village?"

"Absolutely. He was one of the Consortium's strongest advocates."

The intercom on the desk buzzed. "Yes, Molly?"

"Mr. Saunders is on line one, sir."

Harvey Stone lifted the receiver and shielded the mouth-piece.

"Excuse me for a moment. Yes, Saunders." he barked.

"Good. Mmm..." He nodded while drumming his fingers upon the desk. "Vacant possession. Excellent. Keep me informed, won't you?" He replaced the receiver.

"If you are able to assist, I am sure some form of financial arrangement can be made," Harvey Stone continued.

Madeleine sighed. "You just don't understand, do you? We are the pawns, not the players."

"Miss Johnson, I only ask that you exert some influence."

"For financial gain? Don't waste my time."

"Emily?" he asked.

She sat silently. He looked at Ben, who turned his head to the wall.

"If you would bear in mind my offer, I would be grateful."

"I think we should leave now, Mr. Stone." Madeleine rose from her chair.

"You disappoint me. But as you wish. Molly will show you out."

When the door had closed, Harvey Stone picked up the telephone. "I'd like you to page Saunders. Tell him to watch the woman and children closely. And tell him...tell him to be prepared to apprehend them if necessary."

*

In her sleep, Emily's thoughts swirled. They stood at the development models in Harvey Stone's office. He was laughing. He was mocking them.

The village is quite safe, he chuckled.

She peered closely at Island Village, Rottnest. There was movement. Tiny figures were running away from the construction. Tiny Aboriginal people fleeing towards the surrounding ocean, throwing themselves into the water like lemmings. Now she looked at the Greenfields model. There was the same movement of miniature people, fleeing from the buildings. People from Pagan Britain running towards the countryside, horrified at the concrete hell behind them.

Then she saw a group of stationary figures. They wore modern clothes. She gasped. It was David, Madeleine, Ben, and herself. Powerless, helpless. They pointed up to the sky as the first burst of fire rained from the heavens. But the running figures were safe as the model burned. And as the flames consumed the buildings, she saw her own face turn towards her. She awoke with a scream.

"Shh, Em. It's only me."

"What is it, Ben?"

"I've just heard on the news."

"Heard what?"

"Harvey Stone's office. It was gutted by a fire last night."

12

Rottnest Island

From the island, the mainland and distant outline of Perth were clearly visible. A slight haze floated like a shimmering mesh over the city. The Indian Ocean sparkled in the final heat of the day, while the sky changed colour gradually in dipping, twisting bars of gold. It yawned and stretched from a slow, burning orange which poured over the edge of the sky, through crimson and mauve, into coolest azure. The swinging breeze softened the evening like silk, and gently rocked the boats in the harbour. It was the time of day when even the greedy, screeching gulls of Rottnest had retired for the night. The two men drank and talked.

"It's too bad Lewis couldn't be here."

"He was a drunk. I reckon he just got careless."

"Either way, he knew people in the right places."

"This time we're not up against the Wagyl."

"No?"

"The area we plan to develop is a possible Aboriginal burial site."

"Surely they can't be serious?"

"The island was an Aboriginal penal settlement between 1838 and 1903, and apparently a large number of prisoners were buried here."

"So we have the Wagyl at the Brewery site and a pile of old bones here to delay matters!"

"A delay is all it can be. Money and pressure in the correct dosage will restore the patient's health."

"I'll drink to that. Cheers, mate."

A sudden gust of cold air carried from the ocean and caused the men to shiver.

"Did you say something?"

"No, why?"

"It sounded like somebody whispering. I don't know." He shook his head. "Something about creation. *Treat us well or we will return.*"

"Must be the beer."

"Maybe. I'd better have another one, just to make sure."

They laughed. One of the men looked up. "It got dark all of a sudden. Look at the stars out there tonight!"

"Thousands," the other man agreed. "Western Australia is one of the best viewing platforms in the world on a clear night."

"There's a shooting star. Look, it's coming right out of Orion's belt."

"So it is. Something must've annoyed him tonight."

"You're supposed to make a wish."

"I don't believe in that old nonsense."

"I'll make one for you, then. I wish...I wish you'd hurry up and buy the drinks. It's your shout!"

The men laughed and meandered towards the bar. The shooting star continued its descent, streaking across the sky. It glowed as it burned in the atmosphere. Then it seemed to stabilise, and it gathered momentum, causing the air to scream.

With a smack, it hit the ground at the table where the men had been sitting. It landed with such force that it made a crater a metre wide. It lay there, smouldering and singeing the air.

"I've left my wallet on the table."

"Pull the other one..."

"I'll be right back."

The man sniffed the strange air as he wandered back to the table. He stopped in his tracks when he saw the smoking rock.

"Jesus—if we hadn't moved..." He spat at the meteorite, but it was still so hot that the man's spittle evaporated before it could make contact.

There was something on the table beside his wallet. A curious object. It was a head-band. The wind whispered.

"Wear it and be free."

It slipped easily around his forehead. He faced the dark, lapping ocean and smiled. There he was as a child. It was his eighth birthday party, and he was attempting to blow out the candles on his cake. They played pass the parcel. Then the room spun. He smiled again. There was his first car. He had just passed his driving test. The teenage years flew by. Graduation, marriage, first-born. Happy times, achievement. His rise within the Company. The smile vanished. Now came the endless boardroom meetings. Handshakes and back-stabbing; corruption and lies; manipulation and deceit. His marriage crumbled while his career escalated. The projects he had masterminded—bulldozing land and opposition to clear the way for development.

The Island Village file fell on to his desk, and he jumped. Its pages turned. Phase I, Phase II, Phase III.

"Redevelopment, redevelopment!" the wind screamed, and he held his hands to his ears. The head-band felt tight. He tried to remove it, but it felt as though it was fastened to his head. Then he saw the people—sad Aboriginal spirits rising from the ground. Their arms pleaded with him. *"You have betrayed them!"*

"No, no! It isn't true!" The man stumbled towards the figures, but they maintained their distance.

"You have betrayed them!"

"Come here. Please, I can explain!"

He was on the sand now, and stumbling closer to the waves. The head-band clicked tight. Then it began to drill. He screamed and thrashed in the water, forcing his head down as he tried to douse the searing pain. The last vision before his mind exploded was of a man pressing a button on a shiny black box, before the Universe raced by so quickly that the stars became straight lines.

Then the waves washed slowly over him, and carried his body gently out to sea.

13

Visions

Emily gasped. "I was just dreaming about the models burning."

"Dreaming, or being told? You're wearing the head-band."

She looked puzzled. "I don't remember putting it on."

"Em, it's taking over. It's taking us over. I'm not sure that I trust it."

"Ben, you have to. Don't you see? It *is* helping us. This is the Witchetty Men's final warning. There can be no turning back now."

A car horn sounded in the lane. "It's Madeleine," said Ben. "I wonder what she wants so early."

Emily dressed quickly, and they ran to meet her, ignoring their mother's pleas to be civilised and have breakfast.

"What is it, Madeleine?"

"Good morning Emily, Ben. Good news and bad. David has plotted the sequence."

"That's the good news?"

"Yes, Ben. The bad news is that there was another break-in at the Museum last night. The safe was blown open, and the book taken."

"How could they know about it?"

"They have a vision-band, Emily. However, we are still a step ahead...just."

They climbed into the shaking 2CV and headed towards the city again.

"I suppose you heard about the fire."

"I did, Emily. It couldn't have happened to a more deserving man."

"I had a vision of it happening. The models in the room were on fire and people were running away. All except us. We just stood and pointed at the sky."

"Hmm…a glimpse of the future, perhaps. A dream or a vision?"

"I was wearing the head-band. Madeleine, look out!"

She hit the brake pedal and the car swerved, then twitched back on course.

"Heavens, child, what is it?"

"Didn't you see in the road? A great black hole. We passed right over it."

"I didn't see a thing."

"Nor me," Ben agreed.

Emily was still uneasy. "It was there, I swear."

"It may have been a warning to us." Madeleine checked the rear mirror. "The conflict is building steadily. Each day that passes gives rise to increasing turmoil."

*

"That's where I saw the hole in the road."

"You're sure, Emily?"

"Positive."

David looked at Madeleine. "I would say the Witchetty Men have rejected that area for the next circle."

"That leaves us with three sites," she said.

"Here, here, and…here." David rested his fingers on the map. "This has to be the closing circle in the sequence."

"Where is it?" Ben asked.

"Stonehenge."

"I should have known," Madeleine sighed.

"Don't worry for now. It's too obvious a site to pick for the next circle."

"Isn't it a bit obvious to use it at all?"

"I recall a particular passage from the book, Emily." David recited: "…and if we are called from afar, it is possible to meet with the child of the stars at the circle of stones. From our lips, the wind may whisper holocaust. It may also whisper freedom if the time is right."

*

The man entered the circle of stones. In the pre-dawn glimmer, the sky appeared flat. It was as if the tiny ice-fires had compressed it. But he knew that, when the big fire rose, the sky would stretch once more. When it peeped over the edge, the time was right.

The huge slabs pulsed in the mane of fire which tumbled from the edge of the sky. When the beam had been captured, he quickly stepped inside. This time, the light on the head-band crystal did not break up. It remained pure.

"Raise your swords, my men!"

They obeyed, lifting the metal into the beam. It bounced off their blades, creating a circle of criss-crossing, white energy.

The man was triumphant as he lifted his own blade into the light. Then the pictures came to him. Another tribe surrounded the stones, but they were not respectful, for they did not bow down to the fire god. And he spat at them. So hard that they began to spin uncontrollably. When the scene steadied, the fire had gone. The god of cold and iron had spread his icy breath over the land.

"Clavius! Be still," he moaned.

No-one moved.

No-one, save for a small girl who picked her way among the fallen people. But still she did not turn to face him.

The rain came lightly at first. The fire trembled as the sky-splashes thickened. Then the lead gathered, and the fire was extinguished.

"See how our swords have captured the fire!" The man laughed triumphantly. "Test them, my men, for the time for revenge draws near."

Their swords sizzled in the summer rain, yet they were not hot to the touch. Around the stones the men practised. Metal upon metal. The sparks and flash of contact.

The man challenged no-one. He held his sword horizontally. "Ice and fire," he whispered. Then he ran forward, and brought the blade across one of the horizontal slabs of stone. The weapon swished and passed cleanly through. The men stopped abruptly, and watched in awe as the supporting pillars shook and were toppled by the folding-in of the horizontal slab.

"We must return at every moon to safeguard our blades. We have both ice and fire."

"Ice and fire," his men agreed.

When they left the stones, it was with a new energy. An indefinable feeling, somewhere between loss of innocence, and gaining of power.

It was time for revenge.

*

"Today's record high of 38.4 degrees was reached at 2:30. With continuing high pressure, the outlook is for more hot weather. Tomorrow's expected maximum is 39 degrees after an overnight low of 25."

Chief Superintendent Carl Downey scowled at the radio and loosened his tie, so that it hung from his collar like an afterthought.

"Pure coincidence, Laurence. What possible bearing can these deaths have on the accidents here?" He threw the photocopied headlines on to the cluttered desk.

"They report the same retinal damage that was consistent in our cases—the horse, Mr. Gilbert, Miss Daniels."

Carl Downey's face paled at the mention of the librarian. Hers had been a particularly messy suicide. Yet the blindness was consistent, and it frustrated him because it could not be ignored.

"How many deaths in Western Australia?"

"Two that have been reported. One chap was crushed by his four-wheel drive. The other apparently walked into the sea and drowned. Both men had perfect vision, and yet, when their bodies were examined, their retinas had become detached.

"Is foul play suspected?"

"No, but there is speculation that the Wagyl—an Aboriginal Dreamtime serpent—is angry, and that the other Aboriginal spirits have been disturbed on the island where the most recent death occurred."

"Hardly common ground, though, is it? There aren't any Dreamtime serpents here!"

Laurence Bailey shook his head in agreement. "It's worth keeping an eye on though."

"Any news on the fire, Laurence?"

"Arson has been ruled out. The flash-point has been identified as a couple of development models on the top floor. Faulty wiring, flammable material—the usual disregard for safety."

"What are those?"

"They were found in the ashes. The Fire Brigade didn't know how or why they survived."

Laurence Bailey placed a handful of tiny figures on the desk.

"The model family." Carl Downey smiled. "Husband, wife, and two kids." He stood them on his box of matches. "I wonder what they're pointing at."

*

For many days now, the man had painted. It had been a release, almost, to portray what he had experienced. He roasted the goanna over the embers of the fire and surveyed the cave walls. There was the start of his journey. The long walk to the edge of the world where he had waited for the tribe with no substance. Their hollow faces tormented him, but they had to be depicted. There was his spear, left as a warning to the pale ones with no respect. Next came his vision of the spirits rising towards the hand which held the box. Finally, he had drawn the face of the girl again. The longer he looked at her, the calmer he became. She was soothing, although it could be a trick.

When the fire rose the next day, he surveyed his work for the last time. The pictures seemed to live and breathe on the wall. When he left the cave, the heat was already intense, and the sky a dazzle of blue and orange. He drove a spear into the ground at the entrance to the cave and set off. And far behind him, a surging crowd gathered to examine the first spear.

14

Universal Stones

"There's more room in my car," said David. "And, anyway, if someone is looking out for you, they will be expecting a 2CV."

When they left the cool and quiet of the Museum, the humidity of the evening was stifling.

"It seems to be getting hotter every day," Madeleine sighed.

"They are nearly here. The heat is their pressure, their energy approaching. Tonight could be the first flash-point."

"How far is the next circle?" Emily asked.

"About half an hour," David replied, as he eased the car into a lane of slow-moving traffic.

The congestion cleared as they reached the suburbs. Soon they were in country lanes where moths and flies fell like winged rain in the beam of the car headlights.

"The car behind has been following us for miles," said Ben.

David glanced at the rear mirror. He turned into a side road. The car followed. At the next turn off, David switched off the engine and coasted towards the entrance to a field. He flicked off the headlights and they sat in darkness. The other car turned and swished by in the narrow lane. Moments later, it whined in reverse and backed into the same entrance before speeding away in the opposite direction.

"He was looking for us," Ben whispered.

"He?" said Madeleine.

"He or she may have been." David spoke calmly. "We can walk the rest of the way."

Emily savoured the air. It was hot and perfumed. It was also still. So still that sounds travelled easily; country sounds of cattle and sheep. The lonely bark of a dog. And something else. A feeling more than sound—and, though barely perceptible, it drew her towards it. She clasped the head-band.

"This way," she whispered, and they followed in silence, quickly swallowed by the vacuum of the huge field. At intervals, the air and ground grew cold, just as though the warmth had been sucked from them.

"The angel's kiss," Ben thought, as he crossed an area which felt like ice.

David ran a pen-light over a map. "According to my calculations..."

"We're here." Emily pointed to the next field, which swayed with corn as the wind rippled its surface like an ocean filled with shadows.

"Can't you hear it?"

"Hear what?" Madeleine concentrated, but only the rustle of corn reached her ears.

"It's stronger now—a high-pitched whine."

"It could be some kind of homing signal." David looked back. "Damn, they've found us."

Behind them, a convoy of cars turned into the field. Doors slammed. Somebody shouted. Then there was the thud of footsteps.

"Quickly—into the corn," Madeleine ordered.

They fled, and the wind strengthened suddenly, rattling the trees which lined the edge of the field.

"Here will do," Madeleine gasped. "Keep together, and keep your wits about you! It's happening!" She began to chant softly in a tongue which complemented the wind, so that she was barely audible above it. When the corn began to recede, she produced a phial and started to sprinkle the scent of summer flowers. There was movement in the corn. Voices buzzed in the wind. Then the people from the cars crashed into the field. The air was filled with excitement, anticipation, and fear. And the pervading scent of summer flowers.

Madeleine continued to chant until the phial was empty. "Now we must join hands and concentrate on repelling them."

They formed a small circle. Their unity was comforting.

"Close your eyes, everyone. Now, tell us what you see, Emily."

"Space. Stars rushing by faster and faster."

"Repel them. Everybody, will them to slow down. Give us the picture, Emily."

"But how?"

"Just let us in."

"I'm there," said Ben.

"Me too." David nodded.

Together they willed the speeding stars to slow. "Come on," Madeleine urged.

"Someone is interfering." Emily broke from the circle. "Somebody stronger."

At that moment, the corn parted before them, and Ursula, the High Priestess, appeared.

"They come!" she cried triumphantly. Her head-band sparkled. Her eyes were glazed with power and expectation.

"You are a power-hungry fool, Ursula." Madeleine stepped forward. "Return the band before it's too late."

"It is too late. But time passes more slowly while we watch it pass." She smiled.

A dull orange aura lit the night, revealing the grey outlines of hooded heads behind her. They shuffled menacingly closer. Then the corn buckled and bubbled before their eyes, and, as the wind continued to strengthen, the ground boiled and frothed. In a rush of energy, everything peeled away as the circle formed. Then the high-pitched wail deafened them. Except for Emily. She wore the head-band and waited calmly. A beam of light arced into the circle and entered the central jewel in the band. As the corn peeled back, more figures became illuminated. People hiding in the corn, people rushing towards the middle. The air sucked away their cries of terror. A camera flashed, then exploded, burning the hands that held it so that they dripped like wax.

"Take him!" Ursula pointed at one of her cloaked followers. "Take him, I implore you!"

The whine intensified, boring through minds, numbing the conscience. And at the crescendo of the storm within the seething circle, the wind whispered, "*No gain without loss,*" as it lifted the man and then broke him, snapping both his body and his scream.

*

In the furious heat of the Australian sun, Shane Edwards shivered slightly. That was the table at which they had sat, without a care in the world. At least, until Daniels had decided to go for a drunken swim.

He sighed, and looked across the water towards Perth.

"Truly God's own country," he said to himself.

The Island Village scheme had been delayed by the usual petty objections and red tape, but it seemed that at last an agreement would be reached.

"Wave enough money..." He smiled. But he was surprised that Harvey Stone had taken such a keen interest in the scheme. And on a daily basis, at that. There was even the threat of a personal visit. Shane Edwards' smile vanished at the prospect. He had covered his tracks meticulously, but you could never be too sure. He wondered whether Stone could possibly be on to him, then dismissed the notion. It was the scale of the project which had demanded personal intervention. And after all, the amount of money he had allocated for his own use was minimal compared to the overall cost of the scheme.

He dropped to the shore, and ambled across the sand, kicking at the seaweed which was strewn like tangled green hair along the beach. The Rottnest Raider drew alongside the jetty, ready to unload another wave of holidaymakers. The island was immensely popular at this time of year, yet in spite of the crowds, it was still a relaxing place to be. The he noticed something lying in the seaweed. A bright object which was half-buried in the sand. He stooped to pick it up. It looked as though it belonged in a museum. Surely people didn't wear head-bands like this any more! Its stones sparkled in the sunlight. They were truly beautiful. Flashing colours of the spectrum. And one was such a deep, vivid blue that it was like the essence of the ocean. Probably valueless, but worth checking out all the same. He span the head-band idly through his fingers, then continued to plough his way through the golden sand.

*

There was a peculiar calm in the wake of the storm. Although it seemed the world had been flattened by the tempest, people stood still in the moonlight. Nobody moved, and nobody spoke.

Then the wind moaned through the corn, *"That which we have created we may destroy."*

Ursula carved an imaginary semi-circle through the air with her arms. "Come to me, I beseech you!" she cried.

"Tempt us not!" The reply shook the sky and rumbled through the ground.

"Aiee!" Ursula shrieked and ripped the head-band from her forehead. It sizzled when it hit the flattened corn, then bubbled and began to melt.

"Tempt us not!" the voice bellowed again, and to emphasize the command, the heavy heat was ripped apart by a crash of thunder and a stab of lightning. There followed a scream of tearing timber, as a huge oak tree at the edge of the field fell in flames towards the corn. The fire crackled and quickly took hold.

Panic erupted as the flames spread. Figures fled, illuminated by the flickering fire. Figures crying and crashing through the corn.

"Quickly or we'll be fried!" Madeleine led the way across the newly formed circle and away from the flames. Smaller fires started around them, sparked into life by embers carried by the wind from the main fire. The field was being consumed at an alarming rate.

Once, above the roaring inferno, Emily dared to look back. There was nothing but advancing fire and smoke billowing into the sky. And a gowned woman, barely visible. She stood, smiling, in the flames. She pointed at Emily and sneered.

"Ursula?" Emily blinked at the heat and shielded her eyes. The woman had gone.

"Come on, Emily!" David shouted. He led her by the hand, then took over from Madeleine to beat a path forward. The heat and smoke were all around now.

"We're trapped!" Ben yelled. "Can't you help us, Em? You're supposed to be the girl-child."

At that moment, David emerged into an open space. "What the..."

"It's another circle." Madeleine strode towards the centre. She vanished momentarily in the swirling smoke.

"Is it large enough to protect us?" Emily asked.

"I think we'll be safe." David nodded.

The circle was about thirty metres in diameter, with perfectly formed channels which jutted like outer spokes from the circumference of a wheel. They huddled in the centre.

"Safety in numbers," Madeleine whispered. She closed her eyes and recited a prayer under her breath, murmuring while the flames surrounded the new circle. The ring of fire blazed but did not encroach.

"We must lie down to avoid inhaling the smoke," she said softly. "Cover your faces with a handkerchief, clothing, anything. And, Emily, you are to wear the vision-band with pride. It is your destiny, my child." Then she leaned forward, and, to Emily's surprise, kissed her gently on the cheek. It wasn't the kiss of a stranger, nor of a new acquaintance. It was more like a kiss of farewell from a family member, or from a special friend.

They lay face-down, each in silent prayer for the wind that fanned the flames to ease.

Emily began to feel strangely detached from the situation. In the smoke, she began to pick out patterns, just like when she used to play cloud-gazing with Ben. Only here the images were more vivid and believable. Two figures stepped from behind a pile of rubble. Their outstretched arms pleaded.

"What is it? I can't hear you!" She strained to hear the words from their silent mouths. The ghostly figures seemed to repeat the same word.

"It's Clavius!" she concluded.

Then volume accompanied the muted grey lips. "Take heed, girl-child. Take heed of our fate. Clavius' spirits are forever doomed to trawl the dark galaxy; to glide over the ice of a dead world. Anger the Witchetty Men no more to spare the Earth, for their arrival is surely your destruction."

"But what can I do?"

"You are the one. Unite with peace and understanding. Your masters are not without leniency. Our flesh rebelled. Our spirits are now denied the power and passion of our makers. The Keepers from the soil, girl-child. The Keepers from Clavius did the same, and their form returned from the stars. Ten planets to nine. Do not allow nine to to become eight."

"I still don't know what to do. You're talking in riddles!"

"Judgement Day will be at the Stones. The Universal Stones. Be saved, girl-child. Be saved by the power and passion of belief, and humility, for we are all wrong at least some of the time. Act quickly; your world contracts. The Keepers rise in both hemispheres."

"What do you mean?"

"Shh." Both figures placed fingers to their lips.

"Hush now. Call once more; once more we come. Now shelter from the flames and reflect." The smoke rotated and the figures vanished.

15

Kata Kaya

For many days now, an air of expectation had hung over the village. The man watched his people as they prepared, and he nodded in approval. The god of fire had also smiled approval for three moons. The harvest had been the best that he could remember.

From the fires within the mud huts, wisps of smoke drifted into the evening calm, tangling slowly with the aroma from the orchards so that the air was scented like burning cider.

The taming of fire and ice had brought defence in addition to attack. Though the swords of his men seemed invincible, they had fashioned protection from the same metal with shields of plate and leather. The advances had given a buoyancy and confidence not previously known. Most of his men were grateful for the security which the superior metal provided. Some, however, were anxious for revenge, and one man in particular had become intent on attacking the weaker villages. He had already vowed to keep a close eye on the agitator. Now was the time to lead his people into battle.

At the Summoning Drum, they waited patiently for him to speak.

"Kata Kaya—the voice of the eagle—has spoken. The eye of the eagle has seen."

The men murmured and drew a tight circle around him.

"The time is upon us. In two cycles of the fire, we march to the tribe of metal warriors. Revenge, my men, will be swift. As swift as Kata Kaya. There they lie!" He pointed, and all heads turned as though expecting to see the metal warriors.

The man laughed. "Not yet. They are a march of many cycles. But no distance can hide them from us. The gods have blessed us these last three moons. The time is right."

"And what then?" One of his men stood. The agitator was young, but confident beyond his years. Perhaps a future leader, but not yet.

"Then we return, lest we anger the gods. The kiss of cold and iron will soon be upon us."

"Surely we should conquer with our new-found strength?"

There was agreement. The agitator had support.

"The fire and ice was sent for us to avenge the destruction of the village. The eye of the eagle has shown the way. The voice of the eagle will speak again."

"I would like to speak with Kata Kaya myself." The men gasped at the man's blasphemy. "Is there no plan?"

"You would do well to hold your tongue and show the gods some respect. They are our guardians. Now is not the time to incur their wrath. We will concentrate our efforts to defeat the tribe of metal warriors!"

His men voiced their agreement. He still had their support. The young one stood a while longer, then nodded and sat down. But he maintained eye contact. The man nodded also. There sat defiance ready to erupt.

"There shall be a night of feasting before we march, my men. Our voices of victory shall carry far!"

As they dispersed, he made a mental note to give the young one every opportunity to prove himself in battle. Then he smiled. Indeed, the young one could assist him in leading the first assault.

*

By the time the first fire engine could be heard, the field was a charred and smouldering reminder of the fire that had swept through the corn.

"We should leave before they arrive." David brushed the debris from his clothes.

Ben giggled. "Your faces are black! They won't be able to see us anyway!"

"So is yours, Ben." Emily nudged him. "You look like a chimney sweep."

Madeleine remained composed. "David is right. If we are seen, questions will be asked. Come on."

They picked their way through the ash and smoking clumps of withered corn. Each footstep raised a puff of black dust into the air. At the edge of the field, Madeleine turned to look back. She sighed. "It will regenerate in time."

All that remained were the two circles still preserved and clearly visible in the sea of blackness.

"Of course," Emily murmured. "These are the rest of Orion's belt, just like in my dream, when he tipped fire from the sky!"

"Then he has planted the circles which will lead to the final conflict." Madeleine tipped her head upwards, and as they watched, the stars in Orion's belt buckled like blue tears brimming in the sky.

"For two to appear, two have died," said David.

"We saw one man torn apart." Ben shuddered.

"Then someone else must have died in the flames." Emily whispered.

They walked silently away, soon rejoining the lane which led to the car.

*

"...the names of the two dead men have just been released. They are local Councillor Giles Jackson, and Peter Saunders, an employee of Harvey Stone Construction. Our reporter at the scene of last night's blaze is Muriel Thomas."

Their father sat stony faced in the lounge as the reporter took up the story from the edge of the field.

"...and there have been suggestions of a witchcraft link to last night's deaths. Residents will be surprised to learn of Councillor Jackson's involvement with the local coven. Police were only able to confirm the identities of the victims by checking dental records. What is intriguing about the case is the appearance of two more corn circles in the field where the bodies were discovered..."

The news continued from the studio. "With me now are Chief Superintendent Carl Downey and Madeleine Johnson, local spiritualist and corn circle expert."

Ben shot Emily a furtive look. She closed her eyes and placed a finger on her lips.

"...so you see, we are up against a greater power, not necessarily the power of darkness. To a certain degree, mankind has created that."

"Chief Superintendent?"

"We are keeping an open mind, as indeed the police must. No stone will be left unturned during our investigations. We are seeking to interview several persons who were at the scene of the fire."

"You're sure others were involved?"

"Convinced. Several sets of footprints were discovered leading from each of the circles. Two sets in particular concern me because they indicate the presence of children."

"Harvey Stone, of Harvey Stone Construction, today issued a statement expressing his deep regret at the sad loss of Peter Saunders, who he described as 'a valuable asset to the Company, a man who will be missed not only as an exemplary employee, but as a dear friend.'

"The Leader of the local Council paid tribute to Councillor Jackson, who he described as 'a hard-working representative of the electorate, whose expertise, particularly in his capacity as Chairman of the Planning and Development Committee will be much missed.'

"On to the weather, and with temperature records being broken on an almost daily basis, tomorrow's outlook is for continuing hot conditions. A high of 40 degrees is expected, after an overnight low of 26."

*

They were excited at his return from the edge of the world. Many of the tribesmen feared he had fallen off and at first they were wary of his presence. Some even believed he had returned as a spirit, and they prodded him to make sure he was real. When they were satisfied, they settled and listened as he explained the arrival of the tribe with no substance.

To emphasize or clarify certain points, he scraped diagrams in the dust with a stick. When he had finished, they agreed that the best solution was to meet with the pale people.

That night he slept wearing the head-band, hoping for an answer, hoping the Earth would repel the mysterious invaders. There were no answers, but he had a dream about a different tribe with no substance. These men were shorter and more hairy. They were making preparations but for what purpose he could not be sure. Some began to test their spears—not by throwing them, but by stabbing them at each other so that they sparked on contact.

Then he saw the pale invaders again. They were still at the edge of the world, but they had changed its appearance. Trees had been felled and turned into dwellings. Much of the land had been cleared. He saw them hunting, carelessly. And yet their tiny spears found their mark each time. Distance seemed not to matter. He watched in awe as one of the men raised a spear to his face. It flashed and then smouldered. There was something fascinating about its deadly accuracy. There was also something which made him feel more uneasy than before.

16

Keepers of the Soil

"It's a contracting world." David spread the photocopied press cuttings across the coffee table.

The words had a déjà vu effect, as Emily wondered where she had heard them before.

"They are attacking us on both sides." Madeleine frowned as they scanned the articles. "The circle at Merredin is huge."

David nodded. "The *West Australian* was quick to draw a parallel with events here. Look—they've even paraphrased some of your earlier advice, Madeleine."

Ben noticed the picture of Harvey Stone. "All employees of his, I suppose?"

"Not quite," said David. "Two worked for his Australian head office. The others, as I understand it, were involved in negotiating the acquisition of development sites. According to media reports there, circles appeared either at or around the time of the deaths."

"Do we have another Orion?" Emily asked.

"We do." David produced a map of Western Australia. "Exactly the same pattern as here."

Ben checked the star chart. "We're only two circles away from their arrival."

"I've discovered something else which is very interesting," David continued. "The man thrown from the horse near Mr. Gilbert's farm was none other than Harvey Stone's cousin. Apparently the Greenfields development was his vision entirely."

"So Stone lied to us," Ben fumed. "He said Greenfields was a client's proposal and that it was unacceptable."

"He told a half truth. Alex Storey was head of a subsidiary company concerned mainly with identifying potential development areas and drafting proposals. Not the actual bricks-and-mortar approach of Harvey Stone Construction."

"You said he told a half truth?" Emily asked.

"Yes. The Council's Planning and Development Committee approved the Greenfields proposal yesterday afternoon. The Chairman's casting vote decided the application."

"Matters have taken a turn for the worse," Madeleine sighed. "It's time to consult the book again."

"I thought it had been stolen." Ben looked at David and Madeleine in surprise.

She chuckled. "Do you really think we wouldn't keep a copy of something so important?"

As Madeleine spoke, she twisted a blood-red ruby ring on her right hand. There was a click, and a section of the wall behind her slid away to reveal a recess.

"It's a bit like a priest hole." She smiled and disappeared for a moment. "Here." She handed the copy to David. Another twist on the ring, and the wall slid back into place.

Emily noticed Cupid turn, then fire, and reload. "What is he aiming at?"

"The stars." Madeleine half smiled then grew serious. "The spirits are troubling him. He can feel them. He can aim at them. But he cannot hit them, for they are as thin as water, and as invisible as the air that we breathe."

"Our answers lie in these pages." David frowned.

"Or between them," Madeleine said mysteriously.

"Surely, if Harvey Stone is their target, then stopping him is our solution," Ben insisted.

Emily continued to watch as Cupid scanned the garden. He released another arrow. It was deflected immediately, and, as though bouncing from an invisible shield, returned to the grass at his feet.

"It's not just Harvey Stone. It is the folly of mankind."

"Emily is right," Madeleine agreed. "He could simply be a scapegoat for the greed and destruction caused by humanity. Certainly his building schemes have angered them. But there must be something deeper than that. Something sinister perhaps, though I'm not at all sure."

"What else does the book contain, David?" Ben asked.

David continued to frown as he thumbed the pages. "Its themes are similar to those contained in the Bible. Examples set by stories. Guidelines. A sort of blueprint for life, no doubt with additions incorporated throughout history."

"But who wrote it?" Emily wondered.

"It's hard to say," David replied. "I do know that the original had a blank chapter at the very end. We didn't photocopy the blank pages. I ran all sorts of tests in case the text had been hidden by some means. It's as if a final chapter was expected at some stage. This is what I was looking for."

"More maps?" Emily leaned forward to gain a closer look.

"These are the sacred sites. Places where the Witchetty Men placed their spirits on guard. The Keepers of the soil," Madeleine explained.

"The world looks different," said Ben.

"The world *was* different," David began. "The continents were moving, land masses settling. The formation of the planet as we know it has evolved over millions of years."

"Then surely the sacred sites are in different places now," Emily pointed out.

"Exactly. That is why their disturbance has been so difficult to monitor. Over the years, Madeleine and I have tried to anticipate an attack, and of course, the appearance of corn circles is a well-documented worldwide phenomenon. But there was never an identifiable figure from the stars. Not until now."

"Even then, we were unsure how the patterns would evolve," Madeleine continued. "You see, the star patterns we know and easily recognise are no longer in the same place. The light which reaches us is already many thousands of years old, although it hasn't affected Orion's attack. The patterns on the Earth are the same as he appears in the sky, but it will be a dual attack; here and here in Australia," she pointed, "and then here and Stonehenge in the UK."

"What is our next move?" Ben asked.

"I have to take delivery of some artefacts this afternoon," said David.

"And we have a meeting with Harvey Stone," said Madeleine.

"We do?"

Madeline winked. "He'll see us, Emily. You can be sure of it."

*

Shane Edwards pulled another stubby of beer from his esky and toasted his own success. Actually, with Daniels out of the way, any hint of corruption or embezzlement could be conveniently heaped upon the deceased ex-colleague. He smiled a smile of smug self-satisfaction. The alcohol had relaxed him and bolstered his self confidence. He congratulated himself. After all, the saying "dead men tell no tales" could be quite appropriate if Stone did decide to intervene.

As he lay in the sun, the feeling of contentment and well-being, coupled with the soporific effect of an Emu Export six-pack, caused him to drift in and out of consciousness. He was vaguely aware of the sound of the ocean and the screeching gulls which circled overhead. He could smell the saltiness of the air, and feel the sand between his fingers and toes. And he could feel the cold beauty of the head-band as it rested on his stomach. But he did not hear the movement in the cave behind him.

The first shadow that fell on him caused Shane Edwards to stir slightly. When he could no longer feel the sun, he opened his eyes.

93

"What the...?" His words evaporated in disbelief at the sight of several Aboriginals standing over him. He stood up, and they drew even closer.

"Look, if it's about your precious graves, we won't disturb them."

There was silence. He decided they meant business, but how had they singled him out? They were different to the other Aboriginals he had met. He wasn't sure how or why, but they had presence and almost an air of authority. They stared at him and he began to feel trapped and uneasy. Then one of them spoke.

"They are our graves. And those of our Keepers."

"What do you mean?"

"I mean what I say. Now leave us in peace."

The men turned and seemed to melt into the sand.

Shane Edwards shook his head. He knelt to pick up the esky and the head-band.

"Now what do you want?" he said impatiently as another shadow fell at his feet.

When he looked up, the figures were already fading. He shielded his eyes and watched them walk to the water's edge. They were different. Tall, graceful, even. And their heads were almost flat. As he stared, one of the figures turned to face him. He would never forget the featureless face with its red, searing eyes. Shane Edwards' world grew suddenly dark, and he stumbled across the sand, prodding the air with his hands.

"Help! Somebody help me!" he sobbed. And the wind chuckled as it whistled across the ocean.

*

"Don't you see that you are the target?" Madeleine faced Harvey Stone across the desk in his temporary office. His expression remained rigid. Emily thought he looked unwell. His complexion was drained, and as grey as the city walls which nestled in the distance.

"We know about the Australian connection. You've lost Mr. Saunders. It can only be a matter of time," she continued.

"Oh?" Harvey Stone raised his eyebrows.

"It could be you next if you don't leave them alone," Emily insisted.

"Threats, young lady? I have already asked for your assistance. If we can open negotiations, I am sure a satisfactory agreement can be reached."

"Mr. Stone, you really don't understand, do you?" Ben snapped impatiently.

"As I said at our first meeting, I have to keep an open mind. But I really think that what you have told me is the work of—shall we say —a number of fertile imaginations."

"And I suppose we imagined your lies about Greenfields and Rottnest Island." Emily placed the head-band on Harvey Stone's desk. "This could be all that rests between the world and disaster."

"I am a businessman. Revised plans, changes in political climate. These developments are wise investments which will complement the environment, not annihilate it, as you seem to fear. After all, the relevant Planning Authorities have given their approval."

"Unlike the Witchetty Men. Your people are dropping like flies, your office block nearly destroyed. What further evidence do you require of their disapproval?"

"Miss Johnson, I appreciate your concern. But how can I reach a settlement with these Witchetty Men when we cannot even make an appointment to discuss the matter? Until such time as that becomes possible, if you'll excuse me..."

The intercom buzzed. "Yes, Molly, send her straight in, please. My meeting has concluded."

The office door opened, and a woman strode confidently forward.

"Miss Johnson, Emily, Ben, I'd like you to meet Ursula Bishop, my personal assistant."

"Ursula...?" Madeleine gasped in disbelief.

The High Priestess flashed an icy smile and extended a hand, which Madeleine ignored.

Emily reached for the head-band and slipped it around her forehead. Ursula continued to smile, and a whisper carried to Emily's ears: "The Keepers of the Soil are awake."

She turned to Harvey Stone and placed a box file on the desk.

"Molly will show you out. In the meantime, if a meeting can be arranged, please do not hesitate to contact me."

At the door, Emily paused and looked back, whilst Ursula seated herself. She removed a handful of papers from the file, which was headed "CIRCLE HOTEL COMPLEX, STONEHENGE".

*

"Surely Stonehenge can't be developed," said Ben in disbelief, while Madeleine negotiated the impatient, crawling rush-hour traffic.

"Stone is capable of pulling more than a few strings. Without looking at the plans, it's difficult to know what to expect."

"She said the Keepers of the Soil are awake." Emily removed the head-band and shook her hair free.

"That is to be expected. The sequence is nearly complete." Madeleine closed her side door window as she spoke; any relief from the heat had been cancelled by the heavy traffic fumes. "Ursula may have activated them prematurely, but their essence has been troubling Cupid for weeks."

""What does she mean by being awake?" Ben asked.

"They are the next stage in the build up to the arrival of the main party. I suppose you could call them scouts. According to what is written, they have form, though no substance. Their appearance will be shaped by the era in which they were laid to rest."

"Are they dangerous?"

"They are the next link in the downfall of mankind, Ben. If we encounter them, they are to be treated with extreme caution. I expect the main danger will be their confusion at being awoken. They may not know who the enemy is. David may know more."

The traffic thinned and Madeleine opened her window. A stream of country air gushed through the car. Emily closed her eyes and began to daydream. She quickly re-opened them when Madeleine suddenly applied the brakes. Just ahead, a group of men was crossing the road. Small, wiry figures dressed in skins and wielding swords.

"It's the men from the Anglo-Saxon Village," Ben whispered. "What are they doing here?"

"Our first Keepers," Madeleine replied. "It looks as though they are marching to war."

"The ones at the back are different." Emily pointed at the taller, hooded figures. Then the air shimmered and the marching men were gone.

*

The man's eyes twinkled, reflecting the merriment which surrounded him. The people of the village, in varying degrees of sobriety, danced excitedly around the fires. Above two of the fires, a boar and a deer roasted, spitting fat into the flames as they were turned. The lips of evening drew tightly together as the tiny ice-fires came tumbling down, and he marvelled at the figures in the sky. The Hunter, in particular, stood out. The man nodded his thanks, for the harvest and the meat had been exceptional.

When the fire had slipped over the edge, he stood and approached the roasting boar. One of his men sounded the drum, and his people became still and attentive.

"This is a feast to celebrate our future. It is also to thank the gods, and the vision of the eagle. Tomorrow we march. Until then, may the mead flow like water to quench the fire in your bellies!"

He held his sword aloft, then brought it down upon the belly of the beast so that it burst and rained fat into the fire. His people quickly surrounded the boar, tearing out chunks of flesh. Some ripped at it with their bare hands, others dug and gouged with knives. More barrels of mead were rolled from the huts. More laughter rippled the air.

He sat back contentedly in his furs. Through the smoke, his eyes met with those of the young agitator. He had not participated in the feast—that much was obvious—for he was silent and alone. His silence was almost insolence. They continued to stare at each other. Then the young one raised a cup to his lips. When he had tipped the mead down his throat, he shrugged and walked away.

The head-band had yielded no secrets recently. He was philosophical. Surely the lack of guidance meant his leadership was strong and his direction correct. Yet the wind had whispered strange words. He had heard them blow through the circle of stones when they had recharged their swords. He had heard them rustle through the leaves of the oak and beech trees while the squirrels had prepared their winter larder. And he had seen the silent lips of the girl-child form the same word as she stared from the flames of the fire.

"What does it mean?"

He was startled by the voice. It was the young agitator. He had approached with the stealth of a polecat. No-one had drawn so near without detection since he was a boy.

He regained his composure and spoke without turning his head. "What does what mean?"

"I, too, have heard of this holocaust. It troubles me also."

Now the man turned to face the young one. "How have you heard?"

"It is all around. Everywhere I turn, it is breathed."

"Its meaning will be revealed in time."

"I fear time may run out. Is it not a warning from the gods?"

The man watched his people, and he sighed. "The way ahead is clear. That much I do know."

"I have seen the girl. In my dreams." He paused. "But I cannot be sure if they were dreams, for she is real enough to grasp."

"Does she talk with you?"

"No; she barely indicates. Teases, almost. But she holds the answers—of that I am sure."

The man stood. "Have you spoken to anyone of this?"

"Only you."

"Then it is to remain between us, and whatever may lie ahead. Our task is to defeat the metal warriors. There can be no distraction."

They faced each other in the firelight. There was an unspoken understanding, that which occurs when an experience has been shared. Far into the woods, an owl called. There followed a crash and the beating of wings from the silhouetted trees behind them.

"Kata Kaya," the young one said.

The man nodded. "The ears of the eagle have been listening to the tongues which wag like the tails of dogs."

17

Fire and Ice

They stared in silence at the hoarding which marked the entrance to the field. It read, "Greenfields Development Phase I".

"*A tasteful development comprising luxury one, two, and three-bedroom apartments with full amenities.*" Ben read the description with contempt.

Emily turned her attention to the surveyors who measured and pegged. Already, a site office had been erected.

"There won't be any Greenfields left in a few days," she sighed.

"I can't believe Old Gilbert would sell out to developers."

"Times are tough, Ben. He was probably planning to retire."

"Emily, Ben..." The voice startled them.

"Mrs. Gilbert, how are you?"

She shuffled towards them, and her sad eyes blinked at the Greenfields hoarding.

"I'm so sorry. So very sorry."

Emily comforted her. "It wasn't your doing, Mrs. Gilbert."

"But it was! After Pat's death, they put such pressure on me to complete the sale. I signed the papers to stop them harassing me."

"Who were they?" Ben asked.

"Stone's men. One in particular called Saunders. He kept making threats. He said that if I didn't sell the land, the same thing would happen to me..." Her eyes brimmed with tears which began to splash down her face.

She sniffed, then continued. "Pat had called it all off. Something was worrying him."

"Did he say what it was?" Emily asked.

"No, pet. But I think it had something to do with the map. He found this tatty old document in the cellar of the house. Not long after that, he called off the sale. But on the same day, it…happened."

"Could we look at the map, Mrs. Gilbert?"

"I suppose so, Ben, but why should you want to do that?"

"We'd like to see what was troubling Mr. Gilbert."

She turned to the activity in the field. "They were desperate to begin work before the winter, but I didn't expect them to start so soon. This was Pat's favourite field. Fallow this year, corn the next. He often came here on summer evenings to lean against the gate and smoke his pipe." She sighed. "Enough of this. Let's look at the map, shall we?"

They followed the track towards the Gilberts' farmhouse, past the field which contained the first corn circle. Despite the exhausting heat, Emily shivered when they were parallel with it. She glanced to her left. Something moved. Something hovered above the corn. Shimmering shapes hanging and wavering. But it could have been the glare of the sun which pressed relentlessly; so intense that it stifled and mesmerised. She looked away.

"There's no let-up in this weather," Mrs. Gilbert continued. "What we need is a good storm."

They were met at the farmhouse by a large Alsatian which growled menacingly at Emily and Ben.

"Quiet, girl. You remember these two, don't you, Bella?" Mrs. Gilbert soothed the dog. "She's not been herself since Pat passed on. She's been very edgy these past few days."

Ben offered a hand which Bella sniffed suspiciously. She continued to growl softly, and followed them to the back door.

"It's such a bad business, what with Mr. Saunders and the Councillor being discovered. There's gossip in the village and in the news about witchcraft. They've even speculated about my Pat, but it was his heart, you see. Now where did he put it…?"

Mrs. Gilbert began to search the drawers in the kitchen. Emily wrinkled her nose. "You can still smell Old Gilbert's pipe," she whispered.

"What was that, dear? Ah, here it is." She unrolled the parchment on to the table. Ben weighed it down at each end before scrutinising its content. There was silence for a full minute.

"What do you make of it, dear?"

He looked up. "It's a very old map of the village, Mrs. Gilbert. I wonder whether we might borrow it. I know the curator of the Museum and I'm sure he would be interested to look at it."

"Yes, of course. If it's of any historical value, tell him he may keep it," she replied.

At that moment, the gate creaked, and Bella began to bark furiously. Mrs. Gilbert sighed. "There she goes again. Every time the wind tugs at the gate, she thinks we've got visitors."

"We'd better get going, Mrs. Gilbert." Emily rolled up the parchment. "We'll let you know about the map."

"Alright, dear. I'll see you to the gate."

Bella continued to bark as they walked back along the track. Ben was triumphant.

"This is the map."

"I know," Emily agreed. "I couldn't understand all the words, but David and Madeleine will be able to translate them."

"It's the burial site for the Keepers," Ben whispered. "Right here in Old Gilbert's field. Smack bang in the middle of the Greenfields development!"

"No wonder they're not amused with Harvey Stone." Emily stopped. "There's no wind."

"What do you mean?"

"For the gate to swing. There's no wind." As she spoke, Bella gave a loud whimper, and then fell silent.

"I don't know what this map was doing in Old Gilbert's cellar, but he must have realised it would have been dangerous to disturb the Keepers."

"They *have* been disturbed, Ben. And now they are after their map."

Ben shivered when they passed the circle on the way back.

"You felt it too?" Emily asked.

He nodded. "Like fire and ice, Em."

*

They would soon begin their journey to the edge of the world. For some days now, the expectation had been rising like the fire. The elders had voiced both their approval and their caution, and now, while the younger men practised their throwing, he squatted and scratched his thoughts in the ground.

He pondered the great beasts who had roamed and shaped the land. How long they had lain dormant he did not know, but their resting places were all around. He wondered at the tribe with no substance and at the haunting face of the girl who belonged and yet seemed not to belong; so strangely different that she both soothed and troubled him. There were many sunsets to follow, and all would be revealed, for the other men were keen to meet with the pale ones. He scratched and erased, calculating distance and direction. The other men would be able to view his drawings in the caves. They would help him to understand. There was change in the air. A tainted atmosphere. Nothing tangible. He could sense rather than see. But it existed nonetheless, and he felt dilemma in the clarity of that feeling.

As he looked over the land, he was sure he could feel one of the great beasts heave. Just for a moment, the earth quivered and rumbled. In the vast heat, the wind bruised his face. Dust began to rise, and it was then that the trees began to walk towards him.

*

Through her open window, the breathing sounds of night poured. Emily lay awake listening, unable to sleep because of the heat. Distant traffic hissed in the lane. Mournful cattle blew their sad, low monotone across the fields, followed by the shrill cries of bats circling the farmhouse. These sounds of summer were familiar. So too was the sweet fragrance which soaked the air in twists of honeysuckle, jasmine, and roses. But there was something else. Barely audible at first; more a feeling than a sound. Then it became clearer. It was the sound of men shouting. It was the sound of metal upon metal and the cries of conflict.

Emily looked out over the fields, but the moon was obscured, and the night as dark and thick as treacle.

"Em," Ben whispered, "can you hear it?"

"Yes," she replied.

Ben swung into view along the branch of the apple tree. "Get dressed. I want to take a look," he urged.

They were soon both edging towards the ground.

"Look!" Emily pointed at a fire which had started in one of the fields.

"It's in the corn circle!" Ben dropped to the lawn. They ran across the farmland as far as the Greenfields site. Ben rested his back against the trunk of a huge oak. He looked up as he caught his breath, and the height of the tree made him dizzy.

"I can hear them," Emily gasped. "There, look!"

In the adjoining field, a group of men sat around a fire which burned at the centre of the corn circle. One man stood, and as he spoke, the others nodded their heads and voiced their approval. Occasionally, they disagreed, and began to yell and thump the ground with their swords.

Then another man stood. He was tall and fair, and the men were quiet and attentive when he spoke. He walked around the fire, and as he did, he pointed at each of the men in turn, motioning them to stand and speak.

"I'm going to get closer," Ben whispered. "I want to hear what they are saying."

"It could be dangerous. You heard what Madeleine said," Emily replied.

"Come on, Em. For heaven's sake, you're the girl-child; you're special. They can't harm you."

"Our worlds have crossed, Ben. I'm not sure we should be here. Madeleine said they could be confused."

"I only want to get close enough to listen. They won't even know we're here," he insisted.

She sighed in reluctant agreement. Then they began to crawl through the corn. There was a faint rustle and the wind whispered.

"Caution!"

"What did you say, Em?"

"Nothing. Just be careful."

Once, Ben dared to look up, not trusting his sense of direction. He bobbed back into the corn and crawled to the left. Then they sat down in silence while the debate continued.

"Is it not our destiny to arrive at this strange place, my men? We have travelled far, and victory will be ours."

Another spoke. "Your words are like centuries of lead, the darkness of a thousand years."

There were mumbles and more thumping sounds. "Speak not in riddles, young one. State your point."

"My point is this. Yes, it is our destiny to arrive here, but does not one of you remember the battle with the metal warriors?"

There followed a deep silence. "Not one of you?"

"That is why we are here," one of the men answered. "The battle has not yet begun."

"You are right and you are wrong. That battle is over, but the real battle is yet to come. And that is why we are here."

"The young one seeks to bewilder you." The first voice tried to calm the men. "Fear not the enemy without, but the enemy within. With the vision and strength of Kata Kaya, we will conquer."

Emily nudged Ben. "It's them. They follow the eagle god."

"And I say Kata Kaya plays tricks!" the young one argued.

Now the men roared and beat the ground even harder than before.

At length, another spoke. "Show to us some evidence of these tricks!"

"Very well," the man replied.

"I think I've heard enough, Ben. Let's go," Emily whispered.

Suddenly, the corn parted and they were staring at a pair of feet. They were those of the tall, blond man.

"Just as I thought," he chuckled. "Now here's some sport—see this!"

He reached for them, and his hands seemed to pass through their bodies. Emily shuddered as a hand like ice cut through her shoulder. Ben howled in pain as the other hand somehow found a grip and lifted him, kicking, into the air.

"Ha!" the man cried triumphantly. "See how I have this one by the soul! And this one..." He turned to Emily. "This one has no soul."

The men gasped in amazement. "What is this trickery? Look at their strange garments!" They roared with laughter as Ben continued to struggle.

"The young one has mettle," another shouted. "He kicks like an angry woman!"

"Put him down," Emily commanded.

The laughter subsided. In the firelight, she could see the first man's face reveal a glimmer of recognition. Then the blond-haired man began to appear puzzled, as if he too had started to collect his thoughts. He dropped Ben into the corn and looked questioningly at the leader of the men.

"Are we of her time, or is she of ours, I wonder? Come closer, child," he beckoned.

"Careful," the young one cautioned. "She is not quite right. There is something missing from her image."

Emily stepped forward. "I am not afraid," she said.

"Are you a ghost?" the darker haired man asked.

"I think you will find that you are the ghosts," she replied.

The men began to laugh again. "My hand passed clean through her," the young one cried. But when he attempted to demonstrate, Emily side-stepped, and he tripped, face first, into the fire. Yet he emerged unharmed with his features intact. Now the men watched in silent awe.

"It is you who does not burn and drip like wax," she said.

He looked shocked and brushed the embers from his furs. "Is she false, for she does not wear the head-band?"

The older man shook his head. "She is the one. I wonder at her purpose as I have done for many moons. Kata Kaya will reveal all when the time is right."

"When the time is right," a woman's voice spoke from the shadows.

"Madeleine!" Emily turned to greet her.

She stepped neatly into the circle.

"What is this one, a witch?" the blond one spoke. "Is this more trickery?"

The older, dark haired man raised a hand. "Let her speak," he commanded.

"I told you to be on your guard," Madeleine whispered fiercely, "and you," she stared at Ben, "you should know better. Where is the head-band, Emily?"

Emily faltered as she felt for the band. "I must have left it indoors," she replied.

"Enough whispers," the leader grew agitated.

"Apologies, Moi Moi," Madeleine spoke. "Welcome to Shadow-land!" She gazed at the row of faces, examining their features, and her eyes twinkled in the firelight.

"All of you, welcome. But you must now return home. Kata Kaya wishes you well, and bids you a safe journey."

"What is this nonsense? Is this woman bewitched like the young one suggests?" One of the group stood and drew his sword, but the head of the village and the young agitator were still and respectful.

"There can be no fire and ice in Shadowland," Madeleine said firmly.

"Fire and ice," Ben murmured, turning the words over in his mind.

"Fire and ice," Emily repeated, and the sentence swirled from her mouth while Madeleine began to chant. Foreign words, long-lost words. Faint yet alluring. Then the sky tipped and the stars seemed to roll like sweets from a tray. The air buckled and yawned, and in a swirl of angel dust, a hand reached down and plucked the men from the circle.

Just for a second, Emily's eyes met with those of the head of the village. There was a glimmer of understanding which twisted through the mist of centuries. The man raised his sword.

"Fire and ice!" he roared before disappearing.

The fire remained, and it spat and crackled. By its side lay a sword. Ben knelt to pick it up, but it shimmered and glittered into dust. When he stood, the fire had gone.

"At least our Hunter is still with us," Madeleine said. "Come on, let's get you home."

"Thank you, Madeleine," Ben apologised.

She smiled at him. "I know what it is like to be young and adventurous."

"What would they have done with us?" Emily asked.

Madeleine did not reply straight away. She hummed softly as she walked back along the track. "It is nearly time. If they had recognised you they would have probably bowed down in awe. But for now they are returned to their own time."

"But I thought they were Keepers," said Ben. "Spirits, not real people."

Madeleine stopped. "They were both. Something is not quite right. And I fear for their mortal souls. We know that time is for the consumed, and they had been, yet they seemed not to know."

"I'd nearly forgotten!" Ben exclaimed. "We've borrowed a map of the burial grounds. Here." He removed it from his jacket pocket.

Madeleine ran her fingers cautiously across the parchment while Emily explained how it had come into their possession.

"These were no ordinary maps. Here is the treasure, here's twice the treasure, and again." In the moonlight, they stared in wonder as the map changed, time after time, in response to Madeleine's touch.

"Every sacred site on one map. Clever, isn't it? Now we can compare all recorded corn circles with these plans. I'll take it to David immediately. You'll be alright from here?"

They nodded. "How does it work?" Ben asked.

"It's simply a case of understanding the key," Madeleine explained. "I'll show you tomorrow. Meet at my place, eleven o'clock sharp, and I'll drive us to the Museum."

Then she was gone. Hidden by the whispering shadows. Emily looked back as they walked. She could sense something sliding across the sky. And there, gliding past the moon was the silhouette of a figure, arms pointing out from the sides. Emily turned and smiled to herself.

"It's funny," said Ben.

"What is?"

"Madeleine. I didn't hear her car tonight."

"No," said Emily. "She probably didn't drive."

*

The room was strangely cold. Emily shivered as she switched on the light. Then she managed to stifle a scream.

"What are you doing here?"

Ursula sat cross-legged on the bed, with her hands resting, palms upwards, on her knees. And she was wearing the head-band.

"Did I alarm you, child?" She gave a smile like rubies and snow, and her eyes were as cold and emerald-green as those of a prowling feline.

Emily stood with her back pressed against the closed door, and her eyes darted furtively around the room.

"Has the cat got your tongue?" Ursula purred.

"I wasn't expecting..."

"Nobody ever does expect the unexpected." Ursula tugged at the head-band and twisted it idly through her fingers, teasing the metal with her long blood red nails.

"How did you get in, and what do you want?" Emily's fear gave way to anger at having her privacy invaded.

"Never mind the method of my arrival. Now, will you help me?"

"Why should I help you?"

"Don't answer my question with a question!" Ursula snapped. Then she quickly regained her composure. "Emily, there is so much we can achieve. You see, the arrival of the Witchetty Men is not a threat. I see it more as a fulfilment of the destiny of mankind."

"That isn't how Madeleine sees it."

"No, I don't suppose she does. But she is quite wrong. With an appropriate reception, their power may be harnessed."

"And you would misuse that power."

"My child, that is quite wrong. Such a harsh judgement by one of such tender years." Ursula tutted. "They are returning to save the world from mankind."

"Surely they will punish us for harming the Earth."

"They will reprimand, they will snatch technology, and they will delegate their authority to me."

Emily moved away from the door. "What about Clavius? Are we to suffer the same fate?"

Ursula smiled her thin smile. "With your help, we can prevent that. But I need to divert their point of arrival."

"From Stonehenge?"

"That's right. If they don't materialise at the point of maximum power, their strength will be reduced."

"Allowing you to step in. You must be mad." Emily snatched at the head-band, but Ursula's grip was as strong as steel. Their eyes locked in silent combat.

"It is your future, girl-child. Think it over. In the meantime, I'll look after this."

Ursula stepped through the window. The wind rustled her clothes. Then she was gone. All that remained was a hint of perfume. Emily wrinkled her nose and looked outside. For the second time that night, she watched a figure trawl the sky. A silhouette swimming between the tiny ice-fires and gliding out over the moon. This time, however, she did not smile.

*

"I'm afraid the retinal damage is so severe that your condition is inoperable."

Shane Edwards listened to the words without really listening. He had feared the worst, and now the worst was confirmed. He felt detached from the world. A detachment not completely attributable to his sudden blindness. And a feeling of fear and anticipation; a fusion of the known and the unknown. It had gathered and grown since that day on the burning beach.

Fortunately, his position within the Company was secure until completion of the Island Village scheme. Early retirement on the grounds of ill health would net him a sizeable golden handshake together with a comfortable pension. He would continue in a consultant's capacity, and he would continue to divert funds. Shane Edwards smiled at the irony. "What price my vision?" he sighed to himself.

"You're sure there's nothing?"

"I'm sorry, Mr. Edwards," the specialist concluded.

He travelled from one dark world to the next. All were equidistant, for even his perception of time had changed. He couldn't even tell if it was daylight, except that by day the city sounded different and he could feel the warmth of the sun.

Stone had continued to meddle, but even he had seemed impressed at his desire to push the project towards completion.

There had been protests by Aborigines on the island. They had gathered in an attempt to halt the construction. But they had gathered in vain, and he smiled at the not-so-legal methods used to minimise their interference.

He was convinced they were responsible for the sightings of the spirits. One contractor had even claimed to have seen the Wagyl. Probably the result of one too many beers at lunchtime. And anyway, he reasoned, if you believed in that old nonsense, the Wagyl was supposed to have settled at the foot of Mount Eliza.

All the creatures of Dreamtime were supposedly laid to rest. But over the years, sacred sites had been declared by the pressure groups, usually on land involved in development schemes, and on the old Swan Brewery site which was now a protected, derelict eyesore left to decay on the bank of the shimmering Swan River. In Shane Edwards' opinion, the Wagyl had been allowed to wander wherever activists saw fit. But for now at least, the Island Village project was ahead of target, its success marred only by his loss of sight. The burning red eyes of the strange figures on the shore flashed across his mind. Silent, menacing orbs. He was seized by the panic he had felt on the beach where he had stumbled and sobbed in confusion.

"Is everything alright, Mr. Edwards?" the chauffeur enquired.

"Yes, yes," he replied. But he felt far from alright.

18

The Map

"She spoke of diverting the Witchetty Men," Emily explained, as Madeleine drove them to the city. The road unravelled like string while the countryside tumbled by.

"She would harness their power, given the chance," said Madeleine.

"I'd like to know how she got in." Ben leaned forward and placed his head between the front seats.

"Through an obvious door."

"What do you mean?"

Madeleine smiled. "There are doors for some, Ben. And there are doors for others."

"Then she is a witch!"

"Not exactly, Emily. Not in the true sense." Madeleine gave her a knowing wink.

"And what about the head-band—can she use it?"

"Ursula can try. But judging by her previous attempt, I rather suspect the head-band will use her."

At the Museum, David greeted them, but it was with a half-smile which quickly dissolved into a frown.

"They turned the whole place upside-down looking for it."

"*They*, David? Coven or Keepers?" Madeleine cast a disapproving eye over the wrecked displays.

"What use is the map to them?" Ben asked.

"The Book cites the sacred map as the key to uniting the Keepers. The common cause may have been forgotten, so the advance party will seek the others."

"But they are spread over the whole world, aren't they?"

"They are. A spiritual link is all that is required to awaken those that lie dormant. It is vital to keep the map. They must not be allowed to mass. The awakening is inevitable, but we can delay it by withholding this information."

"Did you compare the sites to circles?" Madeleine asked.

"A direct correlation." David nodded. "Every genuine documented circle related to a sacred site. There have been a few hoaxes though." He grinned.

"We kept records of them, just in case," Madeleine explained, "but they didn't fool us. There isn't any feeling or power in the man-made variety."

"And no magnetic field either," David continued. "But now that the sequence is nearly complete, the message to the stars will be loud and clear. It cannot be ignored by the receiver because it is the receiver's message."

Emily walked into one of the rooms. "Do you want a hand clearing up?"

"Thank you, but no. The City Council are deploying some temporary staff to me. It will all have to be pieced back together like a huge jigsaw puzzle."

Two crushed display cases had splintered and merged together. The different tools of different races lay sprawled and confused.

"What does this mean?"

David came to her side. "They are Aboriginal words. Translated, they mean: *'Tribe with no substance'*. Possibly their impression of the first white settlers."

The displays collapsed further. Glass upon wood, stone upon metal. A spear and a firearm made contact, and the noise made Emily jump.

She gasped as a dark trickle ran across the floor. A steady twin flow which spread slowly over the cold mosaic.

David knelt to inspect the tiny rivers, but he knew their source to be the essence of life.

"Is it?"

He nodded. "The blood of ancient conflict. Come on, let's get out of here."

At the doorway, Emily stopped and sniffed the air.

"What is it?"

"I can smell the sea."

As David closed the door, Emily was certain she could hear voices; the far-away cries of men, and the crackle of gunfire. Then the door clicked into place, and the only sounds were those of the restless city and the traffic as it rumbled by.

19

Sky-Swimming

The journey seemed to be taking much longer than he had anticipated. The days were becoming shorter and the nights held the snap of colder air. The trees were all rust and gold and many had begun their autumnal tumble. That morning had been a strange awakening and many of his men were leaden and confused. It was as if they had shared a dream. A dream of another journey to a different world. The young agitator had been most affected, for the experience had placed him in a solemn and pensive mood.

They marched warily and the forest swallowed them. No-one had ever ventured so far in this direction. In their numbers an ambush seemed unlikely, but direct confrontation with the men of another village could not be ruled out.

At dusk they made camp. The forest air circulated cool and fresh, almost bathing them. The trees here were different, still green even in autumn and as tall and straight as the keepers to the gate of beyond.

"I would walk with you, Moi Moi, if I may." The young one approached him. He nodded and picked a path through the trees. The remaining daylight seemed to have been sucked away.

"We should not stray too far from the fires."

"As you wish. Moi Moi, there is destruction in our midst, it lies ahead and behind. It is all around. These strange dreams, this conspiring wilderness. Why does Kata Kaya allow such confusion?"

"It is a feeling within and without. This moment is intended. I do not create our apprehension or our fear. Nor can I dispel the gloom which has settled upon the men."

It became lighter as they walked. The great blanket of kissing trees began to lift. They were in a clearing and overlooking a valley. The fire still stretched its fingers low in the sky. Bars of gold twisted dreamily through shades of blushing pink and cold azure. It was a truly breathtaking fire slip. And as they stared in wonder they realised they had stumbled upon the edge of the world.

"The water touches the sky. And see below; we are above the domain of the metal warriors!"

He looked and saw that it was true. Far below them, wisps of smoke rose from the fires of a village surrounded by a wall of pointed poles. Within the high wall lay other structures and at one end the beasts of the metal warriors were herded. The villagers scurried like ants and their cries could be heard, as could those of the gulls which circled the edge of the world.

"Is there no way in?" he wondered.

There was the clatter of hooves, and a group of men astride their beasts approached the fortress. Their armour glinted in the last flames of the fire and when they were close, the wall lifted and they entered.

"Is that how we are to gain entry?" the young one asked.

"I'm not sure. But I will tell the men we have arrived. Retribution will be as swift as the gulls that harness the air."

Before they had even turned, the strangers were upon them. The air sang with the sound of metal being drawn from the grip of scabbards.

"We have been expecting the king of the savages!" One of the men laughed and lunged his blade at Moi Moi, who sidestepped and flung him over the edge where his lonely scream rose and fell with the screeching of the gulls.

The remaining three warriors closed in with their swords outstretched and prodding as they tested Moi Moi and the young one. Then the fight began in a shower of sparks as metal shrieked against metal. The young one was engaged in single combat, while the other two warriors concentrated their efforts on Moi Moi.

"He fights well for a savage!" one of them cried as he enjoyed the sport.

They were his last words as the blade pierced his armour and his life flowed away on the grass. His last vision was of a sword twisting through the air, and glinting with almost beautiful ferocity. And its cut was the warm and cold kiss of death.

"Just like fire and ice," he reasoned before he fell.

The blade of the young one's attacker snapped so that he clutched only a useless handle. He was soon on his knees and bubbling blood from his mouth.

"Moi Moi!" he cried.

"Stand back!" he commanded. "This will be even."

The warrior inflicted a flesh wound which Moi Moi ignored, though the flow of the crimson tide was great, and it made his arm feel heavy. They stalked and circled each other, and in the final clash of swords, the warrior slumped and gurgled.

Moi Moi stood back. "Fire and ice! See how our metal has pierced their metal!"

The young one wiped his blade upon the grass. "They are many. I wonder at our chances."

Dusk had settled, and the fire had vanished completely. But where it had drowned, the ocean swirled with lingering colour. In the village below, torches lay sprinkled like ice-fires.

"Our way in is to be as one with them."

"What do you mean?"

"To wear the clothing of the warriors is to be accepted as a warrior."

They began to remove the armour from the dead men.

"To gain entry, surely we must master their beasts."

Moi Moi chuckled. "They will be waiting close by. We shall find them."

*

"*...and in our news update this hour, we bring you further reports of disturbances from the village of unrest. Media attention is now focusing on the anticipated arrival of another corn circle, coupled with reported sightings of ghostly figures in the area...*"

David leaned over the desk, and increased the volume of the radio.

"*...late last night, police were called to the farmhouse by a distressed Mrs. Gilbert. Vandals had not only ransacked the property, but blinded the farm guard dog who later had to be put down. Mrs. Gilbert, who was recently widowed, was allowed home earlier this morning after being treated for shock and kept under observation by doctors overnight.*

"*Meanwhile, the Greenfields development has hit problems, and vandals are again to blame. Equipment at the building site has been tampered with and foundation trenches have been re-filled with earth. Harvey Stone Construction has been plagued by difficulties recently, including several employee fatalities, a fire at the city head office and problems abroad. Police are appealing for witnesses to both incidents and are not ruling out a possible link.*

"*Further afield, reports of mysterious figures gliding through the countryside are baffling police and supernatural experts as the media await the appearance of another corn circle in the area. We'll have details in our full news update at 5 p.m.*

"*On to today's weather, and no let-up in the tropical conditions, I'm afraid. Today's high was another record, this time 41 degrees centigrade. After an overnight low of 26 degrees, we can expect a similar high tomorrow.*"

"They are probably grouping in quite large numbers by now." David drummed his fingers on the map.

"I think the time has come," said Madeleine.

"For what?"

"A bird's-eye view, Ben. At night, the Keepers have a distinctive aura. So do the circles, and as the possible sites of the next circles have been calculated, I think we should take a look. The brighter the aura, the nearer the time of arrival."

"How do we achieve a bird's-eye view?"

"You will see, Ben," Madeleine said teasingly. And she gave Emily another knowing wink. "You will both see."

*

In the tumbling light of the full moon, it was a night which could not be dark. They stood at the statue of Cupid.

"Artemis is with us. That is good," said Madeleine.

Emily looked to the moon, locked in the sky like a cup full of dreams. It was so peaceful and hypnotic that she swayed slightly and leaned on Cupid to keep her balance. He rotated without warning and she stumbled on the lawn.

"My, we are touchy tonight." Madeleine stroked his head of cold marble curls. "Now, which way are we to head for our sky-swim?"

The reflection of the moon in Cupid's waterfall rippled as the silver splashes cascaded. Then the garden became bathed in a circle of light which seemed to reach towards the stars. Madeleine smiled and raised her arms. "Kata Kaya and Artemis. On the wings of the eagle, by the light of the moon."

Ben heard a rush of air. Emily sensed that something was with them, but it was everywhere and nowhere.

"See, it's just like swimming. Why don't you try?" Madeleine stretched upwards and rose a few feet. She hovered, treading the air as though it were water.

Suddenly the eagle was with them. Emily heard its cry and felt it soar and swoop. In the blink of its yellow-black eye she was airborne and level with Madeleine. It seemed a strangely natural feeling.

"Come on, Ben. The corridor will soon close!"

He stepped forward and the light made him weightless. When he joined them it lifted and raced to the heavens.

"Which way, Cupid?"

The statue rotated several times like a satellite dish tracking a signal. Then he became still.

"Thank you. Now follow me and keep close, but not too close."

The initial climb as they swam skywards was quite tiring. But when they levelled out it was almost effortless, and each stroke gave increasing speed.

"To change direction, or to reduce speed, paddle with your arms. If you become tired, you can rest by gliding. But if you stop you must remember to tread the air. Otherwise you will drop like a stone, and I can't re-open the corridor tonight."

They followed Madeleine's example. Three figures wrapped in the warm wind, turning across the blue-black net of night, far above the twinkling fairy lights of the village. When the farmland appeared below, a gentle circular glow radiated. They trod the air and watched the circle pulse in luminous shades of amber, pink, and green.

Emily shivered. "The air is like ice."

"Only above each corn circle. They are the cold fury punched through the furnace of destruction," Madeleine replied.

"Look at the smaller lights." Ben pointed at splashes of colour which led from the circle.

"The trail of the Keepers. Come along now—we must catch up."

Madeleine dived to gain speed, and levelled off thirty metres below them. As they followed, they began to experiment. At one point, Ben launched himself into a dive from which he barely recovered. The ground rose to meet the tips of his fingers as he rustled across the top of the corn before gaining height.

Emily hovered above the outstretched limbs of a large oak tree, and Madeleine impatiently watched Ben's dive from a higher vantage point. When he rejoined them, they flew level.

"I can keep an eye on you like this," Madeleine scolded.

The intensity of the trail increased until there appeared a burst of colour on the ground.

"The back-markers. There must be more ahead."

Below them, an army heaved. Its column stretched for as far as they could see, containing ranks of marching figures surrounded by a ghostly aura.

Emily gasped. "There must be thousands!"

Madeleine nodded, and the wind swept back her hair to reveal a worried frown.

"They are massing. See how the columns merge as more join the ranks. They are marching towards the site of the next predicted circle."

There was urgency now in their swim across the sky. The night roared in Ben's ears as he kicked and twisted. To his right lay the lazy sprawl of the city while above him the stars endured, waltzing their patterns through the night. Stars in clusters held by an invisible hand, ready to drop them like sweets. Stars in formation, the tight framework of the Zodiac.

"How far is it, Madeleine?" he asked.

"We follow Orion until it appears. Another five miles, perhaps."

At first it looked like smoke curling towards them. A skyward, drifting trail from the meandering mass below. As they watched, the stream of vapour became a shape—a figure which rippled as it rose.

"Tread the air," Madeleine ordered.

"It's a Clavian!" Emily recognised the sad, gaunt face and the cold, grey lips. When the figure drew level it extended both arms in a pleading, imploring gesture.

"What do you want, wise one?" Madeleine asked. "Have you come to speak with us?"

The eyes brimmed with sorrow. "Many have passed this way. The Keepers swarm," the voice trembled.

"We can see, good spirit. Where are you bound?"

"To trawl the universe. That is my eternal damnation. This planet is too much. There is so much pain, deceit and greed that I am burdened by its weight. So many people and so little time."

The Clavian spirit bowed its head.

"You look like an angel," said Ben.

He looked up, and the grey lips flickered with a smile. "But I am not."

"Is all hope lost?" Madeleine asked.

"It is never lost. They will come to the circle of stones. In both your hemispheres, the Keepers unite and draw the Witchetty Men ever closer. Their arrival is your destruction. Your humility is their forgiveness. She is the one." He inclined his head towards Emily.

Emily remembered the Clavian's advice at the last corn circle. He nodded. "Girl-child, do not allow the nine planets to become eight. Forgive me, but I must leave this misery."

"Wait, please..." Madeleine began, but the spirit was far above their heads and soon out of sight.

"Look, they're stopping." Ben pointed at the collective aura of the army, which had gathered to form a slowly spreading circle with a wall of increasing depth as more Keepers arrived.

"We are here." Madeleine looked to Orion. "We are directly below his belt."

The luminous shapes continued to pour over the ground. Then the centre of the circle began to pulse. Like a beacon, it radiated, growing stronger.

"It's happening," Emily whispered.

The air gave an electric crackle and started to singe. But although the surrounding atmosphere was warm, the air beneath them whispered like an arctic chill.

"We should move away. We're directly above." Madeleine tried to kick away but was restrained.

They tried to move, but an invisible force had locked them in mid-air.

"Don't struggle. Save your energy," Madeleine sighed.

Her words were slurred. Suddenly Emily became giddy. The ground rebounded in focus for one second, blurred the next. Confusion spread, locking their thoughts like lead. Then the sky stretched and the Hunter roared and flexed his muscles. And when the star rolled from his belt, Ben felt a hand of ice pluck him from the sky and send him hurtling towards the ground.

*

The great beasts had been disturbed. They were re-shaping the land again and it was noticeably different during the return journey to the edge of the world. Trees had bowed down to the creature that had passed this way. There were smouldering tears in the ground where its claws had raked. And deep below them, another beast roared and shook the ground as they walked. Two of his tribe had been swallowed while he watched helplessly. Their eyes had been white with fear as the world cracked and spat at them, its huge belly rumbling and drowning their cries. Their legs had been whipped from under them. And then they were gone, and the world had slammed together.

By the time they reached the caves, the land was quiet. The beasts were resting at last. But he was deeply troubled by the fact that they were angry, and he felt guilty at the thought that he may have incurred their wrath. Then he became absorbed by the paintings, and through them his experience was shared. The communication was complete, for his expression through drawing conveyed far more than his words and signs could ever achieve. The figures lived and breathed on the cave walls, and the flicker of the torches gave them an added dimension.

Then he began to understand what was happening. The hand which held the box was far more vivid than he had painted. And next to it the face of the girl had faded. Despite this she was haunting and beautiful. A kind face which smiled slightly, with eyes the summer blue of cornflowers. But she was fading, and here was the conflict. The black figure which held the box was erasing the girl, just as he had erased the people whose spirits he now gathered.

They understood his concern. The conflict, however, involved only the tribe with no substance, for these were the images of the pale people. The strangers on the shore had to be informed, and it was with renewed conviction that they continued to walk to the edge of the world. They did not hear the earth shake at the cave. They did not see the rock shatter as it began its journey towards dust. But he felt as though some of the burden had been lifted.

In the broken cave, the paintings survived. In the darkness, a thin light pulsed from the box as the man's fingers hovered above the button.

*

"Who dares to interrupt our Council?"

A thousand heads were raised as Ben dangled above the circle. The speed of the fall had ripped a cry from his throat. The jolt which jarred his body was not the expected slamming into the ground, but the wrench of a conflicting force which had saved him from the hot and cold touch of the Hunter. The fear had paralysed his voice, and his heart thumped wildly as he hovered above the sea of heads.

"Is this to be the time?" A woman's voice spoke from the gathering. Then Ursula stepped into the circle. "Now will they come to meet me?"

There were murmurs amongst the men, and those without a view of the circle pressed forward in curiosity.

"Are you the one?" a man asked.

"She wears the band, see?" another cried as Ursula swept back her hair.

"Then it must be so."

"No, she is not the girl-child." Ben found his voice.

"What are you, boy? Come down!" one of the Keepers bellowed.

There was growing unrest in the ranks. When the first splashes of rain hit the circle, the ground sizzled.

Ursula looked to the heavens and screamed, "The sky which promised lead shall yield them!"

The elements erupted. The sky and ground exploded and joined as the circle was formed. Energy was drawn and consumed, and the stars blurred as Ben was flung ferociously into the sky, riding the force, propelled by a rush of air and the lash of rain which stung his face and hands.

"*Away, away,*" the wind whispered. "*Stones, fire and ice,*" it hissed.

Emily caught the vision-band and fitted it around her forehead. The elements became calm and they were united in the sky, silently holding hands and looking in awe at the devastation below.

The woodland surrounding the field had been crushed. The debris of broken trees was scattered across the corn. And now there were two circles which were linked, giving the impression of two keys pressed together. Of the Keepers there was not a sign, and all was still but for a garment which flapped idly in the first circle.

"The gown of the High Priestess," Madeleine murmured. "I wonder, have they taken her? Or have they destroyed her?"

"I have the band."

"I know, Emily." She turned to Ben. "I thought we had lost you."

"Did you stop my fall?" he asked.

Madeleine smiled. "It sapped most of my energy. But I think it was worth it, don't you?"

"Thank you. What do we do now?"

She looked at Orion and sighed. "Only one more to tip from his belt. We should visit the stones. I would like to have an idea of when to expect them, although you should feel their arrival Emily."

Emily shuddered. "I can feel something. It's like an energy, inside and out. It's like…"

"It's destiny, and you will feel and you will know. Though I wonder whether they taint the innocent to cleanse the guilty."

They flew as before. Side by side, slipping silently and effortlessly over sleeping towns, far above roads and countryside. Far above the dreams of people.

Madeleine pointed. "Time to go down."

In the orange light they descended to where the stones stood. The sombre grey pillars and slabs; monuments from a pagan past, like guardians of mystery and the solution to the puzzle. A pre-dawn silver glow streaked the sky, with finger tips stretching the horizon and smothering the stars.

The ground within the circle was alive beneath the thin mist which veiled its surface. A luminescent pool of colour swirled and wrapped itself around the base of every stone, beating like a heart of ice.

"The time has come," said Madeleine. "The sequence will be complete."

"How can you be so sure?" asked Ben.

"The intensity. The whole area is charged. They are upon us, and there is nothing I can do to prevent their arrival."

"Can you feel it, Ben?" Emily shivered. "The entire circle is alive and breathing."

At that moment, the first stab of sunlight streaked across the stones. It rebounded, then criss-crossed the circle before dropping into the mist.

"The first beam has to be trapped." Madeleine looked at Emily. "Tomorrow you must catch it with the vision-band. That was the gift of the Old Leaders."

Emily seemed to understand and she nodded.

"Now we must descend," Madeleine continued. "We cannot swim the sky by the light of day."

They dropped gently to the edge of the ring, scooping dew from the grass where they landed. Already the sun had climbed so that where they stood, it seemed to rest on the furthest horizontal slab.

Emily stepped into the ring and the billowing mist hovered above her ankles. "Something is wrong." She turned to face each of the supports.

"What is it?" Madeleine asked gently.

"I can sense betrayal. I can feel destruction. It's old and current. And it's in the future."

A car horn sounded from the road. "That's David, right on time," said Madeleine. She turned to Emily. "This is the strongest of channels. The most open of doors, and the most closed of doors. I'm afraid all we can do now is wait."

*

Shane Edwards could hardly believe the figures. Yet they had been checked and re-checked until there was no doubt. But he still found them hard to accept.

"You're absolutely sure?"

"Yes, sir," his personal assistant replied. "Every account has revealed discrepancies."

"What kind of sum are we talking about?"

"It's too early to know for sure, but certainly in excess of $50 million Australian."

Shane Edwards' face tightened. He wiped the beads of perspiration from his brow and cleared his throat. But his voice still quivered with strain when he spoke.

"That's the majority of our liquid assets."

"Quite. We're still running checks, so I'll keep you informed."

The intercom buzzed. "Mr. Stone is on the line, sir."

Shane Edwards felt his blood chill at the mention of the Managing Director. His mind raced with confusion. He couldn't comprehend how, but he had to accept the reality. Someone was embezzling the Company. Someone who really meant business. And now the finger of blame would point squarely at him.

"...my figures suggest otherwise. The Company could go into liquidation because of this," Stone barked.

"But I fail to understand how..."

"The audit trail leads directly to your office. The transactions have been authorised with your access code. I'm holding you personally responsible, and the authorities..."

Harvey Stone stopped in mid-sentence when he felt the hand on his shoulder. A hand with a grip like fire and ice.

Moments later, Shane Edwards stumbled onto the busy street. The driver didn't react until it was too late. Shane Edwards bounced from the bonnet of the car and was tossed into the air like a rag doll before dropping lifelessly to the ground.

*

"...the discovery of Ursula Bishop's body at the site of the latest corn circle has come at a time when documents allegedly leaked by her suggest fraud and corruption on a massive scale within troubled Stone Construction. With the Company facing the threat of liquidation, work on two major developments, here at the Greenfields site and on Rottnest Island in Western Australia has halted amid rumours of disruption caused by supernatural powers. The Company's latest proposal for the construction of a luxury hotel and leisure complex at Stonehenge has also been put on hold. Outline planning permission has, however, been granted despite a recommendation by the Council's Director of Planning and Development that the application be refused. Councillors last night voted 11–7 in favour of the proposal. The decision has yet to be ratified by full Council. Managing Director Harvey Stone was today unavailable for comment.

"The appearance of another circle and the discovery of a body within has led to further suggestions of witchcraft and occultism. The link between the recent spate of fatalities and Stone Construction is no longer being considered as coincidence and police are today interviewing all of the Company's employees.

"On to today's weather. Continuing extremely hot with the chance of an overnight thunder storm. Tomorrow's high is expected to enter the record books..."

20

The Sequence Is Complete

"There may not be a tomorrow." Madeleine spoke calmly, but her words bore the sting of ice.

"It wouldn't surprise me," said David. "The Witchetty Men will be furious that a proposal to develop Stonehenge should exist, never mind that it should receive approval."

Emily watched the garden. It was a blaze of colour. The borders of flowers which bobbed in the breeze. The lawn still Lincoln green despite the heat wave. A rock garden sprinkled with forget-me-nots which tumbled over the stones like a bright blue waterfall, and Cupid, who continued to pivot and defend his ground.

"He really is confused."

"They are all around, Emily. It is only a matter of time. Even Cupid can't keep the world at bay forever."

"You were going to tell us about the front garden."

"The defences, Ben. Well, since my gargoyle door knocker was stolen, I'm afraid Cupid has had to work overtime. But I'm sure we'll be quite safe for the remainder of the day."

David was studying the map. "I want to be sure we've considered every possibility."

"It will be Stonehenge," said Madeleine. "We have suspected it for years, although I do wonder why..."

He looked up from the map. "Yes?"

"I wonder why they didn't select a very special date. The summer solstice for example."

"It's too obvious. And anyway, tomorrow *is* a very special date."

"I don't see how."

"Today is the seventh of August, 1988."

"Of course," said Emily. "A perfect date. 8.8.88."

As she spoke, the map began to pulse. The sites of the previous circles breathed from the page. And when the final site radiated also, Orion was formed.

"The sequence," said Madeleine, "is complete."

*

They waited on the crystal lawn. Madeleine searched the sky anxiously. "The corridor is late tonight."

The garden rustled. It seemed to respond to her voice. She turned to Cupid and placed a hand on his head. "Thank you, boy," she whispered.

The corridor appeared suddenly, and when it did, Cupid began to turn and fire.

"Quickly, he won't be able to defend us for long."

Ben followed Emily into the sky. Then David, and finally, Madeleine, who sighed as she blew a kiss to the statue before stepping into the pool of light and swimming towards the stars.

Emily felt it first. Like a knife tingling inside her. It was the crack of something brittle snapping. Madeleine knew, and when she looked at Emily, there were tears in her eyes.

In the garden far below them, Cupid lay broken in a pile of shattered marble.

"He is at peace," she said softly. Then with determination. "Come now, there is work to be done."

Without speaking, they assembled in a floating delta formation, with Madeleine at the front, Emily behind her, and David and Ben each at ninety degrees behind Emily.

As they plunged forward, the whole world seemed to turn, and the wind rushed through their ears like water racing through a canyon. Emily looked to the sky, and the sight of scattered stars made her dizzy. Breathless, she stared as the sky buckled and quivered. The myriad cascade of ice-fires shimmered as though an ocean wave had washed over them; blurred but then returning to focus. Far below, the world lay like a brightly dotted sheet. And yet the street lights and city lights waxed and waned.

They were touched by the same wave which threatened to drown all illumination. She looked once more to the dome of the sky, where a thousand cold blue eyes blinked.

"I have never seen a night so beautiful," she thought.

"Beauty can be such a deadly balance," Madeleine replied without speaking.

"How did you...?" Emily began, but then she stopped mid-sentence and smiled when Madeleine glanced quickly over her shoulder.

Tonight there was not a sign of the Keepers. Ben pointed to the brushstrokes on the ground where they had passed.

"They have assembled already!" David shouted.

By now the wind had strengthened and they were buffeted by its warm tempestuous summer breath. The hot fingers pulled at their clothes and tugged their hair. It tried to prise the vision-band from Emily's forehead, and when she lifted her hands to secure it, she lost height which she struggled to regain. And the wind whispered, "*Altricia, Altricia is the holocaust.*"

Emily was puzzled. The words nearly made sense. She was on the verge of understanding them when Madeleine began the descent. Below them, Stonehenge had become an arena surrounded by the Keepers who had gathered in their thousands to await the approach of dawn. To await the return of the Witchetty Men. Their throng stretched far from the hub, their mass of history pressed expectantly against the circle of stones.

"What do we do now?" Ben asked.

"We wait," David replied. "We wait and we pray."

"Can't you feel it?" Emily hovered directly above the circle.

"The hum of expectation. The chant of worship." Madeleine placed a hand on her shoulder. "Do what you can to save our time. My influence here is limited. If fate and the stars go hand in hand, my hand is holding yours for eternity." She leaned forward and kissed Emily on the cheek.

Emily looked up at David. He placed a finger to his lips, then slowly nodded.

"Ben?" she began.

"I know, Em." They looked at each other, eyes flashing like daggers in the dark. Theirs was an understanding which required no words.

The hum around the stones grew steadily stronger. It had a number of components. Tones which affected different senses. A range of lower notes vibrated through the body, like bass beating through the heart. The mid-range clung to their throats, while an upper vibrato, shrill to the ears, entered their heads where it teased and then decayed. The stones began to react, to resonate, and to vibrate like crystal. And as they did, the ground within the circle fell away to reveal the swirling depths of the Earth.

Emily felt the crystals within the vision-band respond with a hiss like snow against glass. And far below, in the gaping abyss, a tiny ice fire appeared. A speck of star which grew in size as the hum of the Keepers rose in pitch.

"*Faster, faster! Onward, onward!*" the wind snarled. Its arrival was unstoppable. The Keepers' fusion with the resonance of the stones was complete and irreversible. With her hands over her ears, Emily screamed, and the stones and crystals echoed her scream. And amid the pain and the wailing crescendo, the star burst from the circle and poured over the stones; and as time and tension twisted, a flashing blade was reversed through the collapsed horizontal slab, and it stood intact once more. In the searing white light, the sky was torn in two, and when the Hunter emerged, he smiled.

"It is time to descend, girl-child. They are waiting for you. Then I will show you the way. Centuries of understanding. Centuries of dust."

Emily blinked away the tears caused by the intensity of the exploding star.

"Orion?"

He continued to smile. "The entire Zodiac awaits." His voice echoed in the silence which had suddenly settled. Emily looked below. The ground had returned to the ring. She took a deep breath and began to descend. Orion threw his hands in the air, and all of the sky shapes bowed down in respect.

The birds started to sing while Emily eased her way down the back of night. Dawn's fluttering eyelashes blinked the stars away.

"The first beam has to be trapped." Madeleine's words meandered through her mind.

She hovered above the centre of the ring, level with the stone which smouldered after its repair.

"The fire and ice have retracted."

"Madeleine?"

"Don't look at them when they arrive."

Emily was level with the sun when it began to climb. Its ascent was the prising-open of the ragged, pink horizon. The golden twists which stretched from the valley of red poured from the spilled cup of fire. The silence was deafening. It seemed that time itself had stopped.

The first ray of the sun slipped over the pillars and entered the head-band. It was immediately distributed amongst the stones. A constant line of captured laser light which was refracted through the band. The circle began to vibrate. Emily felt her head grow warm as the crystals resonated. Her thoughts became molten. There was power within, and power without. Somehow a fusion was taking place; one which both drained her of strength and renewed her energy. To the right, a corridor appeared. She was aware of it but did not turn to look. Instead, she tried to focus on a group of wafer-thin figures who appeared trapped between the pillar and the weight of the sun. They became increasingly faint. Just before they melted away she recognised them. "Of course; they have not returned in time. They would charge their swords but they have failed."

The circle began to spin. Light and sound were united. The arena became one vast stroboscope. She was aware of the Keepers pressing forward in the relentless atmosphere. Something had to give. And when she dared to look down, a man had been flung into the circle. She would never forget the look of terror on his drained grey face. The man was Harvey Stone.

*

As daybreak approached, the horses stamped at the cold which seeped through the sleeping forest. The young one strained to look at the walls of the fortress, but they were still guarded by the darkness which lay as heavy as velvet. The wind hissed at him through the trees, and he shivered beneath the armour.

"We will not move until they are in position," said Moi Moi. His voice was calm and its authority disguised the feeling of doom which had wrapped around his soul during the wilderness hours. It was a feeling he could not dispel, and yet, at this crucial moment, he had to appear the confident leader.

The call of the eagle soared through the valley.

"Is Kata Kaya with us?" the young one asked.

"Kata Kaya has guided us this far. We have mastered these strange beasts. We will conquer the metal warriors."

"They are in position." The wise one pointed to the walls against which his men were pressed.

Moi Moi nodded. "They are poised to spring into action. Come now, my men. It is time for revenge." He kicked at the sides of the stallion, and as they thundered down the hillside, the eagle soared towards the sun. In the blink of an eye, as emotionless as glass, it called. In a flash of flame and gold, it dropped to pounce on its prey.

When the hooves of the horses clattered on the approach to the gate, a small opening appeared.

"Who goes there?"

"We have returned from the forest with news of the King of the Savages."

A pair of eyes flickered in the dark of the recess. "You were in the forest all night?"

"It was necessary. Now we are in need of food and rest."

The eyes examined the four men and their breathless horses. Moments later, a rattle of chains preceded the creaking of the gate as it was opened.

The village was quiet. An early morning mist hovered between the huts. Moi Moi threw back his head-guard to reveal the vision-band which caught the dancing rays of the sun.

"What the...?" The gate-keeper slumped against the wall.

They clattered through the gates of dawn. Then the battle erupted. Men streamed through the gate, and their battle cries awoke the metal warriors who stumbled sleepily from the huts to be cut down by Moi Moi's men. But amid the cries and screams of conflict, a new sound emerged. That of the air being sliced by the tips of steel which rained death on to the battle.

The young agitator was thrown from his stricken horse. "Moi Moi, look over there." He pointed to the end of the fortress where a line of metal warriors were re-loading their crossbows.

"We cannot fight them from here. Even our fire and ice will not reach them. We are betrayed by a secret weapon." In the next flurry of arrows, many of the men were felled and left bleeding in the mud.

Uncaring and unfeeling, the eagle continued to pull apart its prey. Uncompromising talons and beak. The perfect killing machine. In the blink of an eye, it was gone. Lost in the hectic colour of the sky. Calling. Calling daybreak and destruction.

Desolate under the rising sun, Moi Moi tried to retreat. But the chains were closing the gate as the relentless arrows advanced. They were trapped. For those who wore armour, even that was useless. As the last of Moi Moi's men fell, the leader of the metal warriors came forward. And he laughed. "All hail the King of the Savages!"

He drew his sword, and Moi Moi smiled.

"For the power and the glory. To the end, savage. One against one!"

Moi Moi fought furiously but the metal warrior was strong and surprisingly agile beneath his armour. Their swords flashed. Moi Moi's skill with the blade was superior, and yet every strike was deflected. The fire and ice had failed him.

It grows heavier than lead, he thought. Then the metal warrior broke down his guard, and Moi Moi felt his breath run hot.

He laughed. "Now you can feel how superior our metal is, savage." He placed a heavy boot against Moi Moi's chest, and withdrew the sword. The world began to darken. The souls of his men were rising. They were sad.

"Is this not a new beginning?" he wheezed.

"We have been betrayed. Lead us not to Altricia. Lead us not to the holocaust."

Moi Moi coughed as he struggled to breathe. It was becoming very dark. Then he saw the man in black, and he began to understand.

"Is there evil beyond?"

The dark one laughed as he collected the souls, and his finger hovered above the button.

"Don't let him take us. Please, I want to stay." A sea of voices, a torrent of pleas, tormented Moi Moi as he struggled in the mud.

And when the leader of the metal warriors turned to pick his way amongst the fallen men, Moi Moi threw the blade of fire and ice with all the strength he could summon. It flew straight and true, and he knew he had pierced the armour. The voice of the eagle told him it was so.

21

The Witchetty Men

The corridor was as dark as sable. Down it came the hooded figures. So silently, they stepped into the circle of stones.

"Don't look at their faces," Madeleine warned.

There were thirteen cloaked shapes. Thirteen Witchetty Men.

"You are one for each sign of the Zodiac." Orion's voice echoed around the ring. There was silence. "Welcome," he continued.

They threw back their hoods, and there was a gasp as the first line of Keepers were blinded. The red eyes of the Witchetty Men glowed. The light interrupted the ray of sun from the vision-band.

"I can see that all is not well. Is this the one?"

Harvey Stone stumbled around the circle, confused in his dark world.

"Is this an example of what we have nurtured over the centuries? Can this snivelling fool truly represent mankind?"

Emily was seized with a sudden anger at the treatment of Harvey Stone. "Leave him alone. You've blinded the poor man!"

"Ah, girl-child." The icy faces looked to where she hovered. But the scorching eyes, cold as the moon, hotter than bubbling metal, did not harm her. "And you have company. How charming."

"I am not afraid." Emily trembled but her voice was steady. "I have met with you before. I don't know why, or when."

"An element of the stars burns within you, girl-child. We will always remain...bonded, in a sense."

The figure turned its attention once more to Harvey Stone, who by now had backed into one of the pillars where he quivered with fright.

"We can change your future. Or we can end it. Now come to the centre of our beacon so that we may decide what is to be done."

"What will you do to him?"

"This is to be not only his judgement day, but that of the whole planet. Now leave us while we deliberate."

"But you can't try him. You can't be judge and jury."

"Such compassion, girl-child. But that is precisely what we are. Go now."

A hand reached out to her and Orion spoke softly. "I will show you the way."

"Where are we going?"

"You will see."

"But Ben, Madeleine, and David..."

"They are safe for now."

Orion took Emily by the hand and they were swept towards morning as it melted around them. There was a rush of space, a burst of acceleration. The world became a capricious cascade of colour and trembling contours.

"This is spring," the Hunter explained. "Time for renaissance and rebirth." The world was green and fresh and alive with hope and promise.

The seasons unfolded as they flew. Summer smiled, and the air was filled with warmth and honey. Autumn approached, golden and scorched. The leaves tumbled as the breath of the Earth shook them.

Then the world grew cold and dark. They were still. Silence fell like a shroud of ice.

"And this is winter." Emily's words steamed from her mouth.

"This is the eternal winter. This is what would happen."

"I don't understand, Orion."

"Behold Altricia. Behold the holocaust!" He cast the darkness aside to reveal the man in black.

He was hunched over a monitor, buried in feverish activity. The man's eyes were wild with power, his vision distorted by fanaticism. An L.E.D. display counted down the seconds. A shaking hand hovered above the flashing red button.

Emily gasped. "Is this how the world ends?"

"I'm afraid so."

"Can't we do something?"

As if distracted by their conversation, the man turned his head, and Emily faced the eyes which danced with dizzy madness.

She gasped again. "He looks just like Harvey Stone!"

"That is because he is Stone's great, great grandson. The perpetrator of the holocaust."

"But how did he become...?"

"Stone Construction expanded and branched out into post-nuclear physics. The Stone you see before you pioneered the ultimate weapon, capable of wiping out an entire continent in the blink of an eye. And he would use it."

The man's eyes showed a glimmer of recognition as he stared at them. He frowned, then he almost spoke. But then his power-hungry dreams took hold once more. The man shrugged and returned to the screen.

"Final interface. Voice pattern recognised. Two minutes..."

The hand hovered above the button.

22

An Open Door

The edge of the world had changed. It was no wonder the great beasts were angry. The tribe with no substance had carved their own landscape. Trees and bushes had been cleared, and replaced with strange crops and strange animals. Everywhere, it seemed, was dotted with strange structures.

He felt the head-band. What had been revealed to him was true. These people had no respect for the world. They had to be warned of the great beasts' anger. He was determined to tell them of the walking trees and land slips; of the great fire raging inside the belly of the world.

They stepped on to the shore. The edge rolled towards them, licking the salty air and crashing like the sky-drums. He stood where the spear had been planted and let his dreams unfurl. The others joined him, and he shared what he saw. More vessels slid through the water. Many tribes appeared. The landscape continued to change as the pale ones flattened nature. There were buildings taller than the trees they replaced, and great black rivers along which the people travelled. Then there were the huge silver birds with wings that did not beat. And yet they soared and dived like the eagle.

In the dust at the edge of the world, they began to summon the tribe with no substance. And while they danced and called, the pale ones assembled. He kicked and turned in the sand, and advanced towards them, certain that they would understand his approach. As he drew nearer, one of the pale ones clicked his spear and unleashed a crack from the sky-drum.

"Don't come any closer, fellow. We don't want any more trouble from your lot."

The pale one's words were unlike any he had heard before. He began to tell him of the restlessness of the great beasts.

"I'm warning you. The next bullet won't be going skyward."

Encouraged by the man's continued dialogue, he motioned for the others to join him. There would be much to discuss.

"Keep them back, damn you!"

The next crackle of fire from the pale one's spear spat into the sand at his feet.

Perhaps this was their greeting. An exchange of spears between the heads of respective tribes. He raised his own spear and prepared to throw it.

"Fire!" The air was filled with the sound of the pale ones' spears. Their touch was the searing pain of glowing embers. His people's cries accompanied the thunder.

"Again!"

As his body was pumped full of lead, he was comforted by the realisation that the great beasts were not angry at him or his people. They were angry at the appearance of the tribe with no substance. And as he lay twitching in the sand, he realised that Dreamtime was at an end. The voice of the eagle told him that it was so.

*

The sun had climbed higher when they returned to the circle. But today, its roasting intensity was reduced. The heatwave was over.

The leader of the Witchetty Men motioned for them to descend.

"The matter has been settled."

Emily looked at the featureless face. The red eyes burned like fire and ice. She shivered. "What will you do?"

"You have seen the future. You have been shown the past. Without the other, neither can exist. The fate of your world depends on your treatment of it. For now, at least, punishment such as that dealt to Clavius is to be withheld."

Emily heart raced. "Then we are spared."

The eyes glanced at Harvey Stone. "It is not only his destruction of land, and in particular, the sacred sites which angers us. We must prevent an ancestral line which would give rise to the birth of the perpetrator of the holocaust. The man known as Harvey Stone will therefore accompany us on our return to the stars."

Harvey Stone sobbed. "But I've done nothing wrong! Help me! Please don't let them take me away."

The leader of the Witchetty Men continued. "So you see, the risk of our return was not so great as the risk of eventual holocaust. Altricia was the future Stone's vision. But it was a vision only he could enjoy as the lonely ruler of a dead world."

He turned to Orion. "You have watched over them well, Hunter. Now return our Keepers to their resting places. And beware, girl-child. If there is to be a next time, you will not receive one so lenient as Orion. The other sky shapes may not be as kind if they are summoned."

"What should I do now?" she asked.

The burning eyes relaxed momentarily. "The seeds of change are already sown. But the circles will appear from time to time, just to let you know we are still watching. And now you will return the vis-ion-band. There is no need for it any more."

Emily removed the head-band and stepped slowly forward. For a second, they were face-to-face. The cold, white hand brushed against hers as the band was exchanged. Something about the cold face became almost friendly. It was like an inner smile. She stepped back.

The leader of the Witchetty Men raised an arm, and the black corridor extended like a dark comet from the sky. The figures filed silently upwards. The leader paused and looked back.

"Remember, an element of the stars burns within you, girl-child."

He stepped into the corridor, and it snapped shut. Then it raced towards the heavens, until it was no more than a speck of dust floating in the sea of the sky. And the sound of Harvey Stone's screams echoed around the stones.

"Go now, my friends. Return to your rest," Orion commanded. "Even you, knights from the hill. Your work in this time is done. Go with my thanks."

A hum of conversation followed the Hunter's words. The faces that were visible from the circle appeared confused. Orion raised his arms and the Keepers fell silent. A cool breeze began to blow, and on its lips was the whispered scent of summer flowers: the twist of honeysuckle, the haunting aroma of lavender and jasmine, and the climbing embrace of the wild rose. Emily closed her eyes. She thought of Madeleine and her phial and incantations. She dreamed of flying. She felt at one with the eagle as he soared like a golden spirit. All-seeing, all-hearing, all-knowing. "Kata Kaya," she breathed. The ancient eye blinked. The voice called and echoed. When she opened her eyes, the Keepers had gone.

Orion smiled. "My work here is also done. However, there is one last task to be completed." He held a book towards her. "The final chapter, girl-child."

"What do you mean?"

"It is for you to complete. You are to place your right hand on this page, and it will be written. All that has happened here will be recorded."

"But I can't."

"You must. There is barely time. I have to leave in order to take my place in the sky."

Emily took the open book and, without really knowing why, she closed it.

"I can't, Orion. It is not for me to finish what began so long ago."

Orion stepped back a pace. "You disappoint me, girl-child, but as you wish. Though your refusal to write the last chapter has left the door open, I pray that it is not an obvious door."

Orion stood at the centre of the ring. He looked at Emily and nodded his head. Then the sky stretched and kissed the middle of the circle, plucking the Hunter from where he stood. Just for a second, a sprinkle of stars were visible. Blue against blue as the ice-fires arced across the heavens. And as they faded, Madeleine, David, and Ben tumbled into the circle. It was then that the birds started to sing.

23

Cupid's Arrow

"...Harvey Stone's disappearance is the latest occurrence in an extraordinary sequence of events which has seen the Company stagger from one disaster to the next. It is thought to confirm allegations of large-scale fraud and corruption. The Company's latest scheme to redevelop Stonehenge has been postponed, and the planning application which had been recommended for approval before the full meeting of the City Council tonight has been withdrawn. Reports of a disturbance at Stonehenge last night are believed to be connected with protests in relation to the planning application.

"Further documents believed to have been leaked by Harvey Stone's deceased personal assistant Ursula Bishop suggest a change in direction for the Company and an involvement in, amongst many other areas, post-nuclear physics. A spokesman for the Company denies this, or indeed any other change in policy, and insists Stone Construction will continue to build for a better future.

"On to world news, and details of a multi-nation environment summit have been released. The summit, to be held in Brussels next month, aims to discuss solutions to the variety of environmental concerns which have come to light. All nations are expected to be represented. A spokesman today said the feeling of concern was genuine. 'The planet may be a sick patient, and the time has come to call the world doctor.'

"And finally, today's weather. Much cooler than of late. After yesterday's record-breaking high of 42 degrees centigrade, we can expect a more comfortable 25 degrees. Overnight showers are expected. Tomorrow's forecast is for unsettled weather and a top temperature in the low to mid twenties..."

*

"He said the seeds of change had been sown." Emily looked around at the tired faces. Madeleine, in particular, looked drained after the night at the stones.

"For every seed that grows, another must wither," she said.

"What are post-nuclear physics?"

"The next stage in man's quest for power and efficiency," David replied. "I should imagine the difference between nuclear and post-nuclear power would be as pronounced as the difference between the horse and cart and Concorde."

"At least they are meeting to discuss the environment."

"Yes, Emily. They are at last meeting to save the world. But they will never know how close they came to losing it. And we will never know if their concern is genuine or imposed." Madeleine twisted the ring on her finger, and the wall behind her slid away to reveal the hiding-place.

"Time to put these away for safekeeping." She took the Book and the Map from the table.

Emily sighed, and looked to the garden, where Cupid stood intact and still. The first drops of summer rain had begun to fall, rolling like tears from the sky. From the street, the smell of hot dust being dampened filtered through the room.

Madeleine gasped. "I don't believe it!"

David rose quickly. "What's wrong?"

"It's here. Look!"

And when Emily saw what she held, she shivered. It was the vision-band.

"He said we no longer needed it."

"Then this means we still do," Madeleine said softly.

Nobody saw Cupid turn and aim.

Nobody saw the arrow.

Epilogue

They stood alone. Horse and rider at the top of the moon-soaked hill, silent silhouettes beneath the lonely, burning stars. Below them, the lights of the village were strewn. Above them, the ice-fires clung to the net of night as it trawled the sky.

He drew a deep breath, savouring the aroma of summer. The fields of corn wavered and whispered in the breeze which caressed the valley. By the light of the moon, the corn danced in shadows of gold, grey, and green.

The man shivered, and his horse neighed and stamped at the ground. For a moment, the feeling of confidence and success left him. He didn't know why. Then the wind whispered something which caused him to shiver again.

His plans were firmly in motion. He smiled as he looked out over the fields. This would be the final harvest. With planning permission obtained, and a guaranteed market for ellipticinium once mining was underway, the Company's future was secure. More to the point, his future was secure. And with the research team poised to make yet another valuable breakthrough, it appeared they could do no wrong. All the major powers would be bargaining with him for the new breed of weapons.

He laughed, and the sound carried far into the night, far into the fields of whispering corn. A twitch on the reins, and they were off, thundering back down the hillside and sweeping into the sleeping valley. As the ground levelled, the man attempted to pull the horse back, gently at first, but harder in irritation when there was no response. With head down, the horse raced to a gallop, hooves sparking against flints which were scooped and flung into the night. There was terror in both horse and rider now as the fields flashed by. Terror etched in the man's grim face as he gripped so tightly on the reins that his knuckles became white; terror in the wide eyes of the horse as it fled from its invisible tormentors. And there was a madness. A wild, uncontrollable insanity. There was also something strangely familiar in what was happening. The horse had never before bolted, and yet its panic tonight was like an often repeated ritual.

The horse changed direction and crossed a fallow field, rippling the grass which glistened like pearls. He became mesmerised by the moon which rested on the tops of the approaching trees. It was so close that he could almost touch it, and just for a moment he thought he understood what was happening to him.

"No, no!" His colourless face became beaded with perspiration as he continued to struggle for control of the twitching reins. His ears thumped heavily with the sound of his heart and the thud of the hooves. But there was something else. A dark, hollow feeling, and a chilling sound which filled him with horror.

"*Faster, faster,*" the night shouted. "*Faster, faster, onward, onward.*"

Relentless speed.

The man sobbed into the saddle as the fingers of the first branches raked his body, and he screamed when the horse pulled up, throwing him through the air like a broken doll. When he landed, he twitched slightly and screamed no more.

The wind whispered and chuckled. And in the middle of the nearest corn field there appeared a circle.

THE END

ABOUT THE AUTHOR:

Martin Lott is originally from Horley in Surrey. Having spent time living in Perth, Western Australia, he is now a resident of Littlehampton in West Sussex.

42418622R00094

Printed in Poland
by Amazon Fulfillment
Poland Sp. z o.o., Wrocław